THE CANNONEERS
Ben Cross & The Guns of Ticonderoga

Robert W. Walker

THE CANNONEERS
Ben Cross & The Guns of Ticonderoga

DOUBLE DRAGON

From the author of:-

City for Ransom

Shadows in the White City

City of the Absent

Children of Salem

Annie's War

Titanic 2012

Bismarck 2013 – Hitler's Curse

6

CHAPTER ONE

Boston Harbor, November 15, 1775

Hours after the military curfew, sixteen-year-old Benjamin Cross darted from the safety of Gray's shipyard. He'd been crouched among the bundles of flax, barley, rye, and cotton. Seeing his own shadow, thanks to a nearby torchlight, he momentarily wondered if he had any chance at all of escaping the city under British control.

British torches had been planted at intervals all along the dark wharf, and soldiers in gleaming red uniforms, routinely sought out anyone who dared being caught outside past curfew. Two guards marched toward his hiding place, and he must squelch his shadow, so he ducked deeper into the bails and bundles here on the wharf. He felt a sheer terror that his *enemy* would hear his heartbeat and his gasping breath.

Boston's Long Wharf had been his home for as long as Ben could remember, but like everyone in the captured city, he was now trapped. Trapped between two armies since April 19th when British infantry troops clashed with armed Americans at Lexington and Concord. The settlements lay only a few miles from Boston, and as a result of the clashes there and at Bunker Hill, the city remained paralyzed. The population lived under the pale of the months' long siege. The Battle of Bunker Hill had been the last clash, and it had left the two armies in a stalemate for now.

Both armies had suffered heavy casualties, yet no one knew which side had won the battle for Bunker Hill, except to say that the British maintained control of both the city and Boston Harbor, which also meant the shipping lanes. Now with the fighting at a standstill, the Boston Siege as it was being called, had settled into a game of waiting, while most citizens like Ben, who'd been caught up in the war were starving.

The British troops held Boston's citizens hostage to the men they called Rebels, but Ben had heard through the grapevine that the so-called Rebels had formed a proper army, calling it the Continental Army. It seemed more than a rumor or a pretense to Ben, but even so, many Bostonians had long since sided with the British, calling themselves Loyalists…loyal to the King of England and his crown, which had always been the rule in the British colonies here. Regardless, whether a Boston man called himself a Loyalist or not, everyone in captivity here was made to swear the King's Oath of Loyalty; it'd been a decree and carried out in every square and common, but those who'd steadfastly refused to give their oath to the King were hauled off and jailed. Ben and his friend Wilbur Gifford had grudgingly taken the oath, but had done so with fingers crossed behind their backs to offset the lie. Now after nights of preparation and planning, the two young friends had taken steps to end their nightmare and to escape Boston.

Ben Cross scurried on hands and knees through the flickering firelight of the wharf torches, chancing a look over his shoulder for Wilbur, who'd stopped short, frozen with fear, Ben imagined. His own heart was beating like the thumping of a well-shoed horse over cobblestones. Ben's annoyance showed in his handsome face, as he did not want to take a single step backwards in his and Wilbur's movement toward the boats. Still, he must weigh it up.

If Wilbur should be discovered, his own chances of escape plummeted, as they were bound up in this plan as true friends, but Ben knew it was his plan and not Wilbur's, and this was true from the beginning.

His second glance back into the inky night and darkness of the deep shadows cast by the bails, barrels, boxes, and steamer trunks scattered about the wharf sent back no reward. Surely, Wilbur sat frozen in the darkness and was unable to take another step. Ben entertained the thought of going ahead without his best friend, who had been by his side throughout his childhood in Boston.

He ducked low as two armed British soldiers, sharing a single blanket over their shoulders, half-walked, half-trundled on four legs in crablike fashion toward the only heat being given off this cold, damp November night. The twosome looked now like one huge monster, a bearlike creature where they huddled over a fire burning in a barrel. At the same time, the sentries, having set aside their muskets, relaxed, talked, smoked, and flapped their arms for warmth.

Watching the pair as closely as he did, Ben next saw the enemy slapping their arms about themselves to encourage warmth and circulation. As a result, Ben began for the first time to feel the cold that had settled into his bones and flesh. He could hardly make his icy fingers button up the now stiff blue coat he wore. The distance he and Wilbur had come *to-and-through* Gray's Shipyard had already cost him two blistered knees, and now a sliver in his right palm, and him with fingers too cold to pluck it out. Worse still, Wilbur was missing.

The foul odor of fish heads and guts ringed the wharf, mingling with the freshly harvested beaver pelts hung here to dry. The stench of it assaulted Ben's nostrils. Imagining Wilbur caught and executed and hung out to dry, Ben gritted his teeth and began crawling back to where he had last seen his friend. The search did not take but a minute, for there was Wilbur crouched under the shaft of the largest and darkest shadow from a collection of bundled cotton bales.

Ben snatched at Wilbur, pulling at his arm, whispering, "Come on, now! We've a chance, but only now."

Wilbur's round face and wide eyes bespoke his fear. "If-If we're caught, you know they'll jail our parents alongside us."

"But we're not going to be caught. Now come on."

The heftier boy seemed out of breath, afraid to so much as whisper a further reply. Instead, he waved Ben off with a *shoo-fly* gesture and a nod to indicate he was coming up the rear. A soft

November rain had begun to drench the two. It could be a good omen, Ben thought. The rain, while chilling them, would further cover them from the sentries, whose concerns seemed far more for comfort than for duty or guarding this exit by sea from Boston Bay.

They scurried like squirrels past a bevy of emptied rum barrels, the sweet odor hitting them full force. Ben wondered how the wooden barrels had escaped the soldiers, ever in need of more firewood. The soldiers had torn down entire houses that'd belonged to men now enlisted in the Continental Army, using the boards for their cooking fires. Many another home had been invaded instead, taken over, the soldiers bivouacked inside all these months. "Spoils of war" was the term Ben had heard bandied about. The Redcoats had broken shop windows, taking whatever goods they wished, and they'd even scavenged from Mr. Gray's ships, both those afloat and those only half finished ones still in the yard. Ships Ben and Wilbur had formerly been working on as laborers, leaning the craft of ship building.

All for their cursed fires and worse yet, they'd forced Ben, Wilbur, and other boys of their age to help them in their pillaging. After all, 13,000 soldiers needed fires and provisions. Meanwhile, poor old Mr. Gray had been arrested and was living badly, under suspicion of being a Rebel sympathizer on account of his harsh, angry words as he'd watched his shipyard being looted for wood and supplies. *Confiscated* is the word the ranking officer

11

had shouted in Gray's face—so loudly as to lift his beard.

Everyone in Boston was hungry and food was a matter of daily scrounging. The shipment of supplies for the occupying force was a month overdue from England; some feared it had been sunk by a storm, while others wildly accused Rebel forces of somehow placing an explosive on board the cargo ship before it had left Southampton. A story that Wilbur had applauded, but which Ben had derided as far less likely than an Atlantic storm this time of year.

Ben and Wilbur were now out on the long finger of the dock, where they knew a small skiff awaited at the end. They'd seen the small boat used repeatedly by off duty soldiers who had used it to do some fishing in the bay. As they made their way down the length of the dock, each step took them further from the British torches and eyesight. Still, they were hardly out of danger or range of a musket ball. They remained in a crouch, hands and knees still, when Wilbur shouted in pain, alerting the sentries.

Ben turned to see that Wilbur had a huge ugly fish bone sticking from his left hand, with blood gushing. Wilbur gestured for Ben to run for the end of *T-Wharf*. Ben hesitated only a moment, hearing the sentries crying out, "Stop! Who goes there!" and he heard their footsteps closing on them.

"Come on, Wilbur! We can both still make it!" Ben insisted.

But Wilbur shook his head and instead leapt into the bay shallows, the fish bone having been plucked out of his hand by now. In the water, he began splashing and making more noise than an angry sturgeon. Ben immediately realized that Wilbur was in the business now of sacrificing himself so that Ben might make free. So that this gesture would not fail and would have meaning, Ben ran for the open boat at the end of the wharf. As he did so, the two sentries already stood over Wilbur, their muskets cocked and aimed.

Wilbur kept up his noise, shouting, "I fell in! I can't swim! Don't let me die! Please!"

One of the soldiers shouted down to Wilbur, "It's only a few feet there! Just stand up, boy, and you won't drown!"

The other sentry shouted, "Hands over your head! What're you doing out here anyway?"

"Past curfew!" added the other.

While all this was going on, Ben was untying the sailor's knot that held the small boat at the end of the dock. The boat shifted and padded the end of the dock with the movement of the waves lapping at it. Ben quietly slipped onto the boat and began working the oars as silently as possible, a smile creasing his face at the familiar sound of Wilbur's voice as he continued to beg for help from the soldiers. He was now telling themselves that he'd come out here to kill himself so that his mother might have more food in the house for his little sister.

Ben guided the boat due south for the other side of the huge bay and Dorchester Heights, a place overlooking Boston Harbor and Town, and a place occupied by that 'rabble, ragtag rebel army' as the opposition was called by the British officers, who shouted such insults at every drill formation. That was his intention all along, to get to the Continental Army, tell their leaders what he knew of the occupation forces, join up, enlist in the great cause of Freedom for America and American colonists everywhere.

Ben had read all the pamphlets written by the outlaw gang of men who'd started the revolution, and he'd dreamed of a day when all of America would indeed be free of King George's Rule. He knew it was a mad dream, but others his own age had taken up arms to fight for that dream. Now he must do what he could, but the sea had its own ideas as to where it might deposit him, and the harder he rowed for the other side of the bay, the more he realized he was in some sort of powerful swell that wanted its way with the boat, oars or no oars. It soon became apparent that he was rowing in place like a man who'd forgotten to untie the line at the dock, but he was no longer in sight of the dock.

"So where am I?" he asked the empty darkness all around him.

The answer came only when he gave into the sea, upping the oars and planting them perpendicular to the keel. The ocean swells had simply taken on a new life, and they took him in hand, sending the boat to the terrible Back Bay region, a swamp.

Looking back in the distance, seeing that the first grey light of dawn painted the warehouses on Long Wharf and India Wharf beyond, Ben judged the distance from where he had escaped. He hadn't got far, and in fact, he trembled to be so close to where he had boarded the boat to begin with. Beyond the docks, he made out the massive outlines of General Howe's war ships. Angry at his failure to have not gotten any further than he had, Ben pounded a fist into the oar at his left hand when simultaneously a musket ball struck the paddle portion of the oar near his toes now. The ball splintered a hole in the oar. A second shot rang out, putting a hole in the boat's stern.

Ben realized that British soldiers had fanned out along the bay, and that one stood at the end of T-Wharf, having discovered the missing skiff. Not only were the Redcoats onto his escape, they meant to enforce their orders: shoot to kill.

They could not beat the swamp, however. Not any more than Ben could combat it. Still, Ben knew the area better than they did, and he was determined to escape and to live. More shots pinged off the boat, even as Ben slipped over the side, shielding himself. He felt the sea taking him directly into the swamp, as the lightness of morning had begun to seriously cause him problem. Then came the sound of another kind of weapon firing at Ben and he saw the last remnants of fire dancing along the breech of this long rifle. This was followed by a spray of pellets hitting the water and the back of the boat, some zipping past Ben's face. Ben leapt over the side and into the water to the shouts and hurrahs back at the wharf, a few words wafting out to Ben's ears: "I got him! I got the traitor!"

Ben let go of the boat and swam below the water. His body had quickly acclimated to the cold.

He swam, holding his breath for as long as he could. He heard more musket fire as he did so, and he wondered if it was real or imagined at this point. He could not fool himself as to the level of his fear, for another imagining came to mind—his body like flotsam washing ashore amid the seaweed and driftwood. It was then that he heard the bell tolling a general alarm back at the wharf. This made him smile wide.

He took a little pride in himself at the same time as imagining his death since simultaneously he imagined how his little adventure had emptied the Custom's House of Redcoats. It was where so many of the soldiers had been garrisoned. He was a wanted man, wanted dead or alive, he assumed. In his and Wilbur's small way, they had dealt a blow, however slight, to the King's Royal Army.

The marsh was not a safe place to be in at the best of times, and it was far too close to Boston and the Red Coats, who were this minute scouring the area for the escapee. If the soldiers formed a proper search party, he could easily be cut off and captured. He realized that he must keep moving in a southwesterly direction, ever toward the American camp, and even if he could out maneuver the British soldiers, Ben knew there were other dangers lurking in the marshes. Dangers other than the human kind.

His eyes had adjusted to the mammoth field of bulrushes and reeds all around him where he clung to his rock; he knew the big stone was for him an island in a sea of soft, oozy mud and bogs, all just waiting to trap him. Even sure-footed deer were known to get stuck in the quicksand-like bogs here, left to die a slow death. Hunting in the Back Bay area by day was tricky, and men had been known to disappear and never return to their hearth and family, swallowed up by this place. Trying to cross this swamp by night was sheer and utter madness.

"Nothing I can do about it now," he muttered to the night. An owl, safely perched in the trees on dry land, where he'd like to be, replied with its haunting *who-who-who*, which only sent a new shard of fear through to Ben's core.

He wanted to await daylight, but he could hear the Red Coats beating about the shore, and he knew that once they spotted him stuck here, he was a *goner*. He wanted to race for solid ground, but he feared doing that as well. *I'm literally between a rock and a hard place*, he thought, and in his ear, the question of the owl kept sounding—*who-who-who*. But it changed somehow to *here-here-here*, so Ben formulated a plan to take the shortest route from his not so safe perch to the solid ground he sought by making a beeline to the sound of the owl, as that old hoot-owl sure seemed to be telling him to come straight to it and the tree it sat in.

It seemed to be as good a plan as he might devise. He could still see the harbor lights he'd escaped from, and thinking of Wilbur, he feared the terrible punishment poor Wilbur was undergoing at this moment. Then again, perhaps Wilbur was better off than he was. At least Wilbur's fate was decided.

"What's going to happen to me?" he asked the marsh and the owl now.

Thoughts crowded in on him alongside his gnawing hunger. He'd had to take to begging in Boston for crumbs of bread. He'd been abused and disgraced by some soldiers the day before—as had Wilbur and Mr. Gray. Boston had become a bad place, a different and difficult place; not at all home anymore. He missed Wilbur already, and he felt completely alone and on his own, left to his own devices for survival.

In a moment, Ben's resolve to escape went out like the lapping waves around him. Then his resolve returned with the return of the sea striking his little island here. The sea was like a creature with its own heart and pulse, speaking to him, advising him to not give up, not now. He dropped down off the boulder and his feet sank into the sandy bottom beneath the water. He was waist deep in it, and shore now looked like a hundred miles away. Still, he took tentative steps, feeling for solidity below his shoes, a pair of old cobbled castaways with holes in them. The water and sand filled them and tickled his toes with each step toward the sound of the owl.

The oozy floor beneath him threatened to cover his feet and suck the near useless shoes from his feet. Each step felt more threatening than the previous one. It felt as if he might be walking into deeper and deeper ooze of the sort that could take him down. He must swim as far as he could toward shore; he must get his weight off the quicksand below.

Ben tried to swim in as straight a line as possible, keeping his objective in sight, using the coastline as a southerly heading, attempting to let nature help out, allowing the current to take him, hopefully, in a skirting move south of the marshland and bogs. Somewhere behind him now, the owl had gone silent, but ahead, he could hear a definite shoreline as the water lapped against it. Perhaps now the soft, imprisoning muck he'd encountered was behind him.

Then he saw it, an overhanging tree reaching out to him from shore like the hand of a friend. He grabbed onto the branch, its solid bark tearing at him but inviting at the same time. Ben pulled himself the rest of the way to shore going hand over hand, and thanks to the overhanging branch, he found himself on his back, exhausted, looking up at the night sky, panting for breath. The current had taken him several miles below Boston Harbor, and he felt safe for the first time tonight. He closed his eyes, meaning to rest for a short spell when he fell asleep.

CHAPTER TWO

A thunderous clap of repeated gunfire awoke Ben Cross where he slept on the shore of the Back Bay. A predawn twilight had infiltrated the deep woods here, and in the haze of waking, Ben feared the worst—that the Red Coats had tracked him down and were taking pot shots at him here where he lay. But the gunfire had stopped, replaced by the noise of men and animals on the chase, dogs barking, men yelping—not at all like seasoned soldiers. First it was the rustle of the underbrush, then the animal noises, and someone or maybe even two men, seemingly invisible, darting about.

Ben next heard cursing in a British accent, and he saw a single Red Coat stuck in the marsh, up to his thighs in the mud hole. "Over here!" he now shouted, waving his Old Bess rifle overhead, the barrel still smoking from his having fired it. His comrades had fired back in response to alert him to their coming to save him. All this while Ben found cover behind trees in close quarter.

"I've found the runaway! Over here!" the trapped man shouted now. "He's onshore, here!"

Knowing the soldiers must reload their muskets, Ben bolted from the stand of trees toward the hinterland, sure that he must be close to the American freedom fighters and their camp. Behind him, Ben heard the order loud and clear: "Stop! Stop or we'll shoot!" And as Ben kept running, he heard the report of more gunshots, but these were aimed at him. Seconds before the volley, he leapt to the ground, and fortunately no shot struck any part of him but tore into trees all around him.

They were close—closer than ever, he feared. Soon, Ben found himself shaking. He feared the next volley of shots would kill him for sure, when suddenly a war cry like that of an Indian sounded, and it was followed by others just as blood curdling. The whooping and screeching was followed by explosive gunshots right over Ben's head, so close it hurt his ears. At first, he feared he'd been surrounded by those chasing him, but he quickly realized there was a battle between the opposing forces going on and he was in the crossfire! The so-called Rebels were firing at the Red Coats and vice versa.

Ben did not know if the battle was for him or simply for the sake of a battle, when he felt himself roughly grabbed up by a coarse-looking fellow who looked more mountain man than soldier. "Get behind our line, sonny boy! Go!" shouted the long-bearded man. "Go now! Fetch the boy outta here, Ned!"

At the other end of the spectrum, Ben heard one of the Red Coats shout, "Retreat! Back to Boston! Hurry!"

Ben was now in the care of a scarecrow thin character with whiskers and the sharp nose of a hawk. The man called Ned was so well camouflaged in buckskin clothing that Ben marveled at his Native American appearance down to the long, braided hair. He carried a huge knife at his waist along with an Indian warrior club. In his hands, he held his long gun, a hunting musket called a Pennsylvania rifle. The tall man had a hand on Ben's shoulder, and although gunfire blanketed the forest behind them, he casually walked Ben away from the danger while saying, "You look a might worn and hungry, boy."

"I suppose so, sir. I come looking for the American camp that has Boston under siege."

"Well, she ain't much of a siege, but you found us all right. Bet you got some story to tell."

"I escaped, but Wilbur, he got caught."

"Save it for the campfire tonight, son. Gets awful boring being a soldier and all we got at times are card games, tobacco, and campfire stories...with most of 'em being tall tales."

"I can tell you a true tall tale for sure."

"Good...good! Like I said, save it for the campfire, but you can tell it to the captain, and he can tell it to the major, and he can tell it to the general."

The gunfire behind them had become a soft, rolling thunder now as the Red Coats were sent running. A second man in buckskin leggings and coat caught up to them. Ben recognized him as the man who'd plucked him from the earth as if he weighed nothing and shunted him off to Ned. He was broad-shouldered and wider in girth than Ned, and he clearly loved having a reason to shoot at Red Coats. Behind his full, wild beard, Ben saw the smile, and his eyes were smiling too, the crows' feet dancing with his twinkling pupils. "I love a good fight, boys!" he shouted as now all the woodsmen had regrouped around Ben and Ned, all trekking back toward the safety of their own camp. Some had rabbit and squirrel carcasses in hand or slung on hemp over the shoulder. They'd all been out checking their traps when they spotted the Red Coats after Ben Cross.

"Bagged us some interesting game here, Ned," said the big mountain man.

"Sure did, Gill...sure did!"

They laughed and Ben wondered why.

"Just what's needed back at camp," complained a third man in this hunting party. "Another mouth to feed."

Yet another added, "Just another *ragamuffin*!"

Ned said he had to agree with this assessment.

"Weren't you ever a ragamuffin?" Ned replied to this fellow in a defensive tone.

"All's I'm saying is, we don't have *'nuff* supplies, food, and lodging as it is!"

"He's more refugee than ragamuffin," countered Gill. "Still from the look of his clothes, he's gonna need some new duds."

"There's exactly what I'm talking about," said the complaining man.

"Anybody who can bust out of Boston, Effram," began Gill, "that fellas a friend of mine. He's likely got lots to tell the *muckity-mucks* about what's going on down there in the city."

"However did you escape that place, anyhow, boy?" asked Ned.

"Name's Ben...Ben Cross, sir, and I...well, I took a row boat, but they shot holes in it, and I had to take to the water and pray a lot."

"You musta wanted out of there pretty badly," remarked Gill.

"Yes, sir. I was hoping to join up with the Rebels to fight for Boston."

"You like starvation and lice, do ya, boy?" asked the one called Effram. Then they all laughed again.

"We'll take the refugee to the new general's tent," said Gill.

"That fellow named Washington?" asked Ned.

"One and the same, Ned. A general oughta know what to do with him."

"You're gonna bother a busy general with this whelp?" asked Effram.

Gill stopped in his tracks and turned to Effram and took a fighting stance. "This boy's got eyes and ears; he might well have valuable news for our leaders, Effram. You don't know otherwise, now do you?"

Ned quickly agreed, standing with Gill and saying, "The boy's important, Effram."

Ben had never heard himself called important in all his life.

"Oh...now we get to the truth Corporal Gill McCleary!" shouted Effram for all of them to hear.

"What're you bellowing about, Effram Shanley? Have I ever...ever pulled rank on any of you boys?"

Effram scrunched up his features at Ned and Gill. "You two...damn it, Gill, if you ever make sergeant, it's gonna go to your head."

"Is that what this is about, Effram?"

24

"No...no, it is about the boy. He don't look like no prize to me."

Some of the men laughed at this. Gill took a step back from Effram, easing off. Ned followed suit. Effram pushed it, adding, "Pretty obvious you hope to curry favor with the new general, Gill, maybe Ned, too, so's you'll look the hero and be ranked upwards."

"Effram, you want to get ahead in this new army, you're going about it all wrong. If you want to take the boy here to the general, be my guest."

Ben was fast coming to feel like a pawn on a chess board in some game these men were playing out. Effram backed off, waving a hand in the air, out of words it seemed. "Nah, you fellas take care of the boy—and feed him, and clothe him, and bunk him like he was your own for all I care, but don't be taking any of my rations."

When they resumed walking toward the America lines again, it was in silence until Ned nearly whispered to Gill. "What're we doing here, Gill? We oughta be someplace where there's some *gall-dern* fighting going on!"

"Well *dag-nabbit*, Ned, it galls me too, sitting around like we are, but there's no cure for it in sight."

"Nothing's happening here but hunger and a waste of time, and it's poisoning our friends like Effram against us."

"Fighting could commence here anytime, Ned. Why, we just run off a passel of Red Coats just now, didn't we? They're coming out to fight and soon."

25

"Real fighting's going to break out up north and along the Champlain and Hudson Rivers, Gill. Upper New York! We should've joined up with them Green Mountain Boys headed up *that-a-ways*!"

Gill McCleary hitched up his buckskin pants with one hand, held his musket over his shoulder with his other, and sighed before saying, "Ned Bottomly, listen to me now. Not sugar coating a thing, one of the reasons we're in this war is the history of our Irish and Scottish forefathers with the British. Now we've come to a new land, a land of the free, and here they are again with their king— *not ours*—wanting to lord it over on us. I say we stand with this fella Washington."

"Why, Gill? What's he done?"

"He's tall in the saddle is why; he can pull this disorganized army into something that just might work. Besides, I like the cut of his uniform. Did you see that uniform?" Gill laughed as Ned pondered this. "Seriously, Ned, I tell you, this Washington fella from Virginia, he's got the backing of the Continental Congress, and these are leaders who're gonna pull this *dust up* of ours into an organized *war*. You just mark my words."

Ned looked from Gill to Ben, staring. "I sure hope you're right, Gill. Ben, I look forward to your campfire story tonight. For now, I guess we go find the general's tent."

Ned Bottomly set the pace with Ben and Corporal Gill McCleary bringing up the rear. "I want to thank you men for saving my hide back there."

The men made no reply as if they did not hear his words. Ben could only guess what fate had in store for him next. He momentarily wondered if this General Washington was anything like the British fellow, General Howe. Ben had never heard the name Washington. No one in Boston went by that name. He imagined Washington would likely be a lot like Ned and Gill.

"Ethan Allen!" Ned erupted, repeating the name several times. "Now there's a leader of men. A man who figures out his objective, knows what results he wants, takes aim, and goes after it! A man of action, Gill."

"Ohhh, I sure have heard of him," Ben piped up.

Ned looked over his shoulder at Ben, a lopsided grin creasing his features. "The boy's got smarts, Gill. See what I mean about Captain Allen? The man's already a legend, taking a whole fort away from the British like he done!"

"Yeah, real impressive man, for sure," agreed Gill.

"He's fighting while we're all sitting around, playing cards, fighting among ourselves, squirrel hunting, all these weeks without a single shot fired!"

"Ned, the way I heard it, Captain Ethan Allen took Fort Ticonderoga up in northern New York without firing a shot. Took the British completely by surprise and let them march out of the country and into Canada."

"Where they belong!"

"This here…what we got here in Boston, needing to take a whole city—and not just a fort—it's just going to take time, and besides, we need artillery before we can do it."

"Cannons! Who needs cannons?" Ned countered. "We've got more men than they do. I say we storm across Boston Neck and be done with 'em!"

"Okay, General Bottomly." Gill laughed again. Ben had never met a man given to more laughter than Gill McCleary.

Suddenly a huge blast exploded over Dorchester Heights, where they were headed, where the American camp stood. The British cannons in Boston, placed on Bunker Hill, began firing their morning volleys. Their guns could not reach the heights, but their cannon fire could not reach the top of the Heights, so that when Ben Cross entered the camp with his newfound friends, he found the camp laughing and jeering at the British guns.

Another explosion two thirds of the way up the Heights sounded awful but did no harm except to the geography of the hillside. "Here we go again," Ned muttered. "Some war. We get this and talk, talk, and more talk."

"Mr. Knox says different, Ned."

"What does Knox know?"

"A lot about cannons is what. He says if Cambridge and the Heights could be properly fortified with cannon, we'd have us a proper siege, and we'd have Boston and her harbor back in our hands in a matter of days if not hours."

"All they do is talk about what ifs, while they got us digging trenches and sandbagging fortifications. It ain't proper work for a real soldier."

"Do you see any real soldiers around here?" Gill was losing patience with Ned. "Look, Mr. Knox has read all the books on conducting warfare, and he knows more about breastworks, fortifications, and cannons. It's why General Washington listens to him."

"Knox?" asked Ben, interrupting the buckskin soldiers. "It's not Mr. Henry Knox of Boston, you're speaking of, is it?"

"You know him, son?" asked Gill.

"From Boston, yes! He owns the bookstore on North Street."

"Bookstore?" asked Ned. "He's got all his *training* from books?" Ned began to laugh now. "I *knew* it...knew there was something you couldn't trust about that big man."

"Hold on," said Ben. "Mr. Knox, he was a member of the Train."

"Train?"

"Militia of Boston, sir. An artillery unit, and he was in charge of it last I heard."

"You hear that, Ned? In charge of an artillery unit. Ben, how many guns...ahhh cannons did the Train have and where the hell are they?"

"They only had one 20-pounder, sir."

Ned erupted in laughter again. "A militia artillery unit with one cannon. Did they have only one cannon ball, too? Har-har!"

"You didn't let me finish," said Ben. "They also had three 3-pounders. All of them were confiscated by the British right off. But Mr. Knox led a band to steal some of General Howe's cannons. It failed 'cause they couldn't find a way to sneak them out of the city past the blockades, but Mr. Knox, he knows all there is to know about cannons. I went to school with his brother, William. Wilbur and me and Willie were all good friends."

Ned remained skeptical. "A Boston bookseller, ha!"

"Mr. Bottomly, he sold paper, quills, ink, and he did some printing as well as selling books."

"There's your war expert, Gill," Ned said, rubbing it in. "A paper expert. Lord help this poor excuse for a rebellion. It's been put in the hands of a gentleman farmer of Virginia and a bookseller of Massachusetts."

Ned marched off and away from Ben and Gill, laughter in his wake. Gill looked at Ben for a moment and frowned. "Pay no attention to Ned and Effram and the rest of 'em. They've all had a rough time of it here and are all out of sorts. Once you get to know all of the men, you'll fit right, in Ben. Now exactly how old are you, for when I introduce you to General Washington? First thing he'll want to know is if you're old enough to carry a rifle into battle."

CHAPTER THREE

The center of the Rebel camp was neither the Heights nor Cambridge so far a Gill knew, as at least till now, he was told, it remained Roxbury. As a result, Ben followed Gill to General Washington's headquarters there. What Ben noticed here as elsewhere was the absence of *flags*—there were none. By comparison, the British had draped Boston with the Union Jack from top to bottom. The army that had chased the King's men from Lexington and Concord, and had fought so bravely at Bunker Hill, did not appear to have a flag.

Proper uniforms were just as scarce, or so it seemed. Most of these soldiers wore the clothes they plowed fields in—or as with Ned and Gill—hunted in. On foot, without provisions, many carrying rusty, seldom used squirrel guns, the American Army looked as sad as a shipload of ragged famine victims that Ben had once seen come in on a ship in the harbor.

Ben's keen blue eyes saw that the disorder at Cambridge and here at Roxbury had some order to it after all. Some sections of the camp were attached to inns and mills, where companies were bivouacked both inside and around the buildings. Some details worked on digging latrines, while others drilled under the orders and shouts of sergeants and lieutenants. Other small groups sat busily cleaning weapons or peeling potatoes.

Looking all around as they neared their final destination, Ben failed to see the taut rope and stake that caught his ankle until it sent him toppling over to the delight of anyone close enough to see. Laughter erupted, and Ben, while embarrassed, decided that laughter appeared to be the only steady nourishment these men had.

Inside the tent where Ben had fallen, he heard two men hardly laughing; instead, they were shouting at one another, so caught up in their disagreement that they paid Ben's prostrate body no mind at all. Ben quickly got to his feet and still the two arguing men seemed to not see him. He began swiping the worst of the dust from himself, when he realized his clothes were still caked with the dried mud from his overnight stay in the Back Bay bogs. He felt a rush of embarrassment at his appearance as he realized the two men in disagreement were officers, and in his ear Gill said, "That's General Washington and your old friend, Knox going at it again."

"What're they arguing about?"

"Cannons…what else?"

Just then, the tallest man that Ben had ever seen stormed out of the tent, leaving Henry Knox pacing in a little circle. Gill called out to General Washington, but he kept walking, got on a white horse, and rode off in the direction of Cambridge.

Knox stuck his head from his tent and called to Gill, saying, "Corporal, who've you got with you here?" And as soon as he said it, Henry Knox's eyes brightened on seeing that it was Ben. "Ben? Ben Cross? Is that you?"

"It's me, Mr. Knox, sure is!"

"I thought you were in Boston."

"The boy escaped last night, sir," Gill said.

Knox grabbed Ben up in a bear hug, "Well this is a great how do ya do? What about William? Is he all right?"

"He's had a bad cold and a fever, sir. He wanted to escape with me and Wilbur, but he wasn't in no shape to try."

"What happened then to Wilbur?"

"Caught...he created a diversion so's I could make it out."

"We found Red Coats chasing him this morning and ran them off, Mr. Knox."

"Well now, the general's going to want to hear any news you have from inside the city, Ben."

"Yes, sir, but he just run off." Ben pointed in the direction Washington had taken.

"They've set up a new headquarters for the general at Harvard University," Knox explained. "We can all go together. I'll see that you gain his attention."

"I'm sure he's got lots on his mind," replied Ben.

Knox, a large, rotund man, smiled wide at this. "You have no idea."

As they neared Cambridge Commons on foot, Ben watched several units of riflemen marching back and forth in awkward rows; the men startled some cows at pasture, and the cows began mooing in response and now were running ahead of Gill, Knox, and Ben. With the cows returning to grazing,

33

Ben recalled how often he'd watched Henry Knox and other Bostonians march up and down the streets of the city in British uniforms at the time, as acting militia in His Majesty's service, a service they called "The Train" before the outbreak of hostilities.

Knox's company had also trained on British made artillery. It had been general knowledge that when the fighting broke out in Lexington and Concord, Henry Knox was offered a highly prized commission in the British artillery. Instead, Knox had fled Boston by night, apparently before every exit was guarded. Some in Boston believed that he had kept on running, calling him a coward, a fool, and every other name imaginable. Ben knew now that he had not run any further than to the American side of the conflict.

Harvard University loomed over everything here, and Knox pointed a finger at the college, saying, "There's the general's headquarters. Ben stared up at the huge, brick building, the sound of soldiers marching and shouting all around him. Here he saw more uniforms belonging to militia companies in Vermont, New Jersey, Rhode Island, New York, and New Hampshire where Ned and Gill had come from, according to Gill.

Most of the uniforms that Ben saw on the backs of soldiers here in Cambridge—other than the roughhewn clothes of volunteers like Gill—were British issue with a few modifications. The colors of the Massachusetts Militiamen, many of whom had trained with Knox. Other colors no doubt had come from militiamen who'd arrived from Virginia with Washington, New Jersey, and the other surrounding colonies. Nowadays, they were no longer separate militia companies but the fighting arm of the Committee of Safety as it was being called, the same committee that had begun in response to the *Boston Massacre*, some five years ago now. Rumor had it that Henry Knox had been at the Boston Massacre, where he lost a finger on his left hand. It was also said that he had been among the cooler voices that day and had helped bring the riot to an end.

After the first American fatalities that day in Boston five years ago, Knox had become more and more a mediator between British officials and the colonists. Some saw him in those days as a concerned citizen the same as John Adams, while others characterized Knox and Adams as collaborators on the side of the British.

So much had happened since Ben had become a prisoner in his own city. He'd heard of this man Washington, as had every colonist. After all, George Washington had distinguished himself in the French and Indian War. The British takeover of Boston was to be the jumping off point in the War of the American Rebellion brought on by the Continental Congress. This 'Rebel Parliament', as the British called it, had established its Continental Army, the same as the British called the 'Rebel Army'. This Rebel Congress had recently placed George Washington in charge of the combined forces of the American colonies. His task was to build a real army of fighting men from all the thirteen colonies—each with its own generals and officers.

Until now, Ben had seen very little of this side of the battle lines that had been forged to cut off anyone coming or going into Boston. Until recently, the conflict had been called "a farmer's revolt" and "soon to be put down" by British authorities and General Howe in particular. For Ben, seeing the size of the American camp now in three separate locations, the "farmer's revolt" took on a whole new meaning. It was certainly more than a band of angry farmers. At least here in Massachusetts, the revolt had become a full-on Rebellion and a War for Independence as all thirteen colonies were rallying to the cry for freedom from the tyrannical yoke of King George of Great Britain.

Harvard was the largest building other than Boston's North Church that Ben had ever seen; it rivaled the warehouses on the wharves as well. Entering the halls gave Ben a chill; they were so large and the ceilings so high. The guards knew Knox well and waved them through on sight of Henry. As they neared Washington's office, they could hear him inside, shouting still. This time he was saying to some of his officers, "No, there is no dropping our weapons and returning to the fold, not now, not ever! Are you blind? A British takeover of our largest seaport and city, and now an American force has taken a British fort in Ticonderoga in Upstate New York? Gentlemen, we are at war; not at games here."

"But there's been no...no formal declaration of war from the British," countered another voice in the room, where Knox had Ben and Gill settle themselves onto a bench.

Washington's booming voice replied, "I've heard all about the bargain Howe hoped to make with the Committee of Safety from Henry Knox, and we must reject it, gentlemen. If their actions and our actions at Ticonderoga, Lexington, and Concord before that is not a declaration of war, then what is?"

Henry Knox opened the door and stepped through it. In the next few minutes, uniformed officers filed out of the room one by one, each speaking to the others in mixed grumblings. Then Henry cued Gill and Ben to enter.

Washington came to Gill, shook his hand, and then did likewise with Ben. "I understand you had a skirmish with Red Coats this morning and saved this boy from them, Corporal McCleary."

"Yes, sir...but I had help of six of my men, sir."

"And Ben Cross, Henry tells me you've come straight from Boston. We need you to tell us how things in the city are."

"Are, sir?"

"How life is going for the people quarantined there."

"Oh...it's bad, sir...very bad."

"Can you tell us how bad? Details, son."

"Awful bad, sir. The Brits, they didn't just take over the city and harbor, sir...but more than that."

Washington indicated a chair for his guests. "Go on, Ben."

"The Red Coats have burned most of the houses."

37

"Burned the houses? We've seen no such fires."

"They take down a house or a business—like they did with your bookstore, Mr. Knox—board by board, and they use the wood for their campfires and to stay warm, sir."

"*Ahhh*...I see, so they're burning the homes, yes?"

"Started with the businesses of anyone they thought disloyal to the King, sir."

"What else can you tell us, Ben?"

"For firewood they destroyed most of the shops and Mr. Gray's entire inventory at the lumber yard. His warehouse is only still standing 'cause they're using it to house soldiers. Poor Mr. Gray's lost everything. I was apprentice to him, you know. Was learning how to make cabinets and furniture and such as that."

"Disruption of life," muttered Knox, picturing his Boston as it must look now.

"They took some awful delight in using your books, Mr. Knox, as kindling for their fires."

This news seemed like an arrow to Knox's heart. Washington shook his head. "Burning a single book is a shameful act, let alone all those books. *Horrible.*"

"I hate to imagine what they would do with the library here, sir," replied Knox, "should they take this position. We desperately need those cannons, and I know I can deliver them by springtime, and the Red Coats are not likely to make much trouble in the winter months, and they won't have any inkling of a clue as to our plans and battlements with the first thaw."

Washington stood and paced and went to the window and nervously thrummed his fingers on the window sill and stared out all at once. Not one movement of his huge frame was wasted or rested while he was in deep thought. Ben could hardly take his eyes off the giant in the room. The general was two heads taller than Knox.

"Corporal McCleary here and his New Hampshire boys, sir, they are willing and able to shoulder the load right through winter," said Knox now. "I have the men and equipment lined up and ready to go, all just waiting for your orders, General, sir."

Washington went to a map of the entire eastern seaboard that had been hastily tacked to one wall. Knox joined him, and the two men began mapping out a route to Fort Ticonderoga from Cambridge, a route that would serve Knox both ways—if the mission was approved. "There're so many river crossing and so much timber in your path, Henry."

"These men are trail-blazers, sir; they have opened up all manner of wilderness. They can sit here all winter and add to your troubles and desertion rate, or—or we can give them work to be done—to bring home to Boston the captured arsenal of cannons at Fort Ticonderoga.

Ben immediately wanted in on this adventure. He had all his life believed that he was meant for far more than hanging about the wharves, or building cabinets for ship interiors in Gray's lumber yard, and this mission that Knox had proposed to

Washington to fetch the guns of Ticonderoga to bring to bear on the British in Boston and Boston harbor sounded like a gift to Ben's ears. He kept mum, however, knowing that he'd have to bide his time to somehow convince Henry Knox that he, like the Vermont mountain men, had it in him to be of service on such a mission.

Gill had stood and gone to the map to point out some areas that he was familiar with, demonstrating his worth to the mission. Ben had never been out of Boston, and he had no idea how he might convince these men that he, too, should be on this mission. He had involuntarily stood and joined the men at the map. He gasped at the distance they were speaking of. The fort in question stood at the bend in a river that ran from Canada, near the top most tier of the New York Colony. It was well over three hundred and eighty miles (380) from Cambridge and Boston, and they were talking about making the trip with oxen pulling huge pallets and wagons over rocky forested areas where not so much as an Indian footpath existed, traversing waterfalls and rivers frozen over in mid-winter, not to mention hundreds of broken gullies, crooked dips, slippery rocks, natural and manmade stonewall obstacles, slides, shoots, and snarls.

"We can do it, General, sir," Gill promised. "My men would much, much prefer going for the guns and hauling 'em back here for your pleasure, sir, than sitting out this winter twiddling their thumbs and tamping their growling bellies, sir!"

"That's precisely what we all want, sir," began Knox, completing his marks on the map with Gill's corrections. "We've talked it over among the men. We all want to place a full complement of artillery ordnance into your hands, General, to see what we can do about the damnable enemy once we have that fire power, sir. Put your and my book learning to the test."

"Mr. Gray always says, 'right tool for the right job'," added Ben.

Washington looked at Ben as if he'd forgotten he was in the room. "Smart man, your Mr. Gray."

"Taught me how to build anything—even if there're no nails. The Red Coats took all his nails, too, for fear they'd be stolen and used in scatter guns against them."

"You can build things of wood, Ben, without nails?"

"Old fashioned way, yes, with wooden pegs. I can repair just about anything too."

"Good…good, we can always use another carpenter in camp," Washington said. "Gill…I want you to find Ben here a place to stay and I bet he's not eaten for a while."

"Yes, sir, General." Gill saluted and took Ben by the arm, guiding him out. In his ear, he said, "Time to let Mr. Knox take it from here."

When they got outside the room and began traversing the hall for the guarded doors, Ben said to Gill, "Sure is strange, the general's uniform."

"Strange he even has one in this man's army," replied Gill.

Washington was wearing a blue and buff uniform with gold braiding and a red sash. He'd looked dashing, so tall and erect, and how he filled

41

that big room, Ben had no idea. Knox was also a big man. Big in girth and across the chest and shoulders, and in his way just as imposing a figure as was Washington. Ben had never seen Knox so in charge and so sure of himself before now.

"You realize that was the newly appointed Commander-in-Chief of the newly fashioned Continental Army, Ben, that you just met. I only met him myself the other day when Mr. Knox insisted I tell him that my New Hampshire fighters are ready and able to do what Washington was, at the time, calling impossible."

"Going for the guns at Ticonderoga, you mean? Gill…I want to go with you and the men; I want to be a part of this mission."

"That's crazy, son."

"But Gill, you're going to have breakdowns for sure; you are going to need somebody who can fix problems fast—and I have blacksmith and woodworking experience, and I'm good with animals. They like me!"

"Well I like you too, son! If no other regiment will have ya, I reckon we'll have to induct ya. How old are ya, again?"

"Seventeen, sir."

"That's old age given the times. When time comes, I'll see to it you're sworn in proper."

Ben smiled at the thought of being a part of this man's army.

CHAPTER FOUR

That night around the campfire, Ben was encouraged by Ned Bottomly to tell all the New Hampshire men how he had escaped Boston. Ben found he had no need to embellish a word of his story, that it was exciting enough and harrowing enough—just as it happened moment by moment. The retelling left him sad, however, even as the rough and rustic men of the New Hampshire Ninth cheered, for the story had reminded him of Wilbur's plight. He'd gone to bed with this on his mind, and it'd made for troubled sleep, despite how exhausted he was from the day's events.

Then he was awakened early by a series of rooster crows and bugles being blown. Each division and regiment had its own bugler, and each felt it his duty to blow the wretched thing. Ben had no experience with waking up so early, and it took successive blasts on the bugles to get him to turn over when he heard Gill shouting and then felt him shoving him into consciousness. "The general and Knox want to see us, Ben. On the double!"

Ben found a water barrel and threw some water in his face and toweled off, but Gill gave him not a moment more to get his bearings. "Now, son!" He dragged Ben off toward Harvard Hall. Ben was as yet only half awake when they entered Washington's office at the center of the university. It appeared that the faculty and the president had long since vacated the premises. It was rumored the president was a Tory, who stood firmly with the "rule of law and King George".

Knox and Washington had a breakfast of biscuits and gravy awaiting Gill and Ben. The four of them sat about a former conference table, enjoying the meager but welcomed food. Hot tea was also poured. General Washington wasted no time, getting right to the point.

"Ben, my boy, we're interested in just what sort of conditions the British soldiers and officers are faced with in Boston."

"Conditions, sir?"

"Food for example and fresh water…how are their stores?"

"Not good, sir. They were hoping for a ship to arrive with more provisions, but it's weeks late, sir, and they're taking livestock and food wherever they can steal—confiscate it, they call it."

"Sounds like they could be getting desperate."

"Hunkered down, sir. They don't care for the cold, these soldiers, and like I said, they're tearing down shops and houses to burn for warmth. Boston Common's covered with tents like you got outside here, sir."

"What about the food that is available to the soldiers, Ben?" asked Knox. "Do they have oranges, fruit?"

"Not hardly, no."

"Vegetables?"

Ben shook his head. "They weren't too smart about stretching what they stole, sir."

"Well then what are they eating?"

"Mostly gruel."

"Gruel? What sort of gruel?"

"Watery gruel…soup flavored with leather, sir."

"Are you sure of this?"

"Well the officers, they seem to have better soups and breads."

"How do you know this, Ben?" pressed Knox.

Ben shrugged, hesitating over his breakfast, his mouth half full. He spoke around the food in his mouth. "That's all the soldiers talk about—how the officers are eating better than them. That and how cold they are."

"This is good news for our side," said Knox, smiling and looking at Washington, who nodded knowingly.

"So they have no meat, and we have cows to last us through most of the winter," Washington now said, sipping at his tea. "You know an army fights on its belly."

"They get rice and beans from the warehouses, though," added Ben. "They get cornbread, fish when they can get it." Ben patted his stomach. "Guess I've lost twenty pounds myself. Used to be as fat as your brother, William, Mr. Knox."

Ben saw the anguish on Knox's face at the mention of his brother.

"William's really alright, sir. He's not in no danger. I worry 'bout my friend Wilbur far more. Not sure what they might've done to him for his helping me to escape."

They all fell silent over their breakfasts for a time, until Washington said to Knox, "Sounds like they aren't any better rationed than we are."

45

Knox nodded and replied, "Not hardly, if Ben's account is even close."

Ben muttered, "I hope I may never see another potato as long as I live."

"They can't hold out forever. No army can march on cornbread and gruel."

"Still, without proper artillery, General, we are at a stalemate, and in no position to storm Boston either. You must hold your position, sir, and we both know this."

Washington drew in a long breath of air as if to clear his mind. Ben thought he looked tired, as if he hadn't slept. "Sense dictates I hold, Henry, yes...but wars are not won on common sense alone. No, if the rabbit does not soon leave his lair, we must drive him from it."

"The rabbit must wait until we can blow him from his lair."

Ben wondered what rabbit they were talking about until Gill said, "General Howe sure has been acting like a rabbit. He'll wait for that next ship to come in from England before he comes out after us."

Washington tossed his napkin down and stood. He paced the room. "No one, not the Congress, not the other generals, not my officers, and not my own men will long tolerate this waiting game, Henry. Gill tells me that every day we are having more desertions from the ranks."

"You have to forget about General Lee's letter to Congress, sir!" Knox exploded. "You cannot attack now, not without artillery, sir. Your men will be cut to pieces. I believe Lee wants your job, sir."

"And he will have it if the Congress agrees with him."

"We both know that a loss here at Boston would spell disaster for our cause; it would mean an end to any hope this army has of becoming a fighting force, sir, and of this country's ever being free of England."

Ben dared not look up from his biscuits and gravy; he felt certain that the general would be angry with Mr. Knox for his outburst, but then he heard Washington laughing. He looked up to see that the general was smiling at Knox. "I like a man who expresses himself with such fervor and fury, Henry!"

"I'm sure it helps that you know I am not just full of sound and fury, but that I am right!"

Washington continued to smile. "You are good for my heart, Henry. Well said, quoting Shakespeare back at me."

"Let me lead an expedition to Fort Ticonderoga, sir, please. I promise that I can supply you with a full contingent of artillery by Christmas Day."

"Now wouldn't that be a Christmas gift!"

"I swear it, General."

Gill said from his seat, "We can do it, General. I know we can."

"Infectious notion you have, Henry. Do your men know what back-breaking work it was to build the Pyramids of Egypt?"

Ben as well as the others stared at the general, curious about what he meant, when Washington added, "Dragging cannon over frozen land and the deep snows of northern New York will be like building the pyramids."

"I know that country up there, General," Gill defended.

"So you know it's over three hundred miles of the roughest terrain you will ever encounter. Much of it has not been surveyed or even mapped. I know this on account of I was there fighting the French and Indians."

"No matter, sir," said Knox, following Washington around his desk as if in pursuit. "We—you—desperately need those cannons, sir!"

"Henry, we do not even know how many cannons there *are* at that fort."

"With a full complement of British soldiers manning the fort, it is surely a sizeable number, but our not knowing is just more cause for me to go up there and catalogue and dismantle for transport the entire ordinance for the Continental Army, sir. To bring it to bear on General Howe's defenses here, sir!"

"All right, Henry, very well, but only on one condition."

Knox's features pinched in confusion. "What condition?"

"I'll agree to this mad scheme of yours Only if you will accept a special commission as my field marshal in charge of artillery, Henry."

Knox smiled widely. "Done!"

The men again went to the maps, this time maps spread across Washington desk, and they began to study them closely, still trying to determine the best route to and from Ticonderoga.

"I don't envy you men; I've been to the Berkshires, and Ticonderoga requires you to go smack through that wilderness. You'll be halfway up the Hudson River Valley. No telling what obstacles you'll run into…from the weather, storms, the land, and things that live on the land—from bears to Indians."

"We'll take extra supplies to trade with any chiefs we run into," said Knox.

"You have an answer for everything, don't you, Henry?"

"It's the only way to win a war, sir."

"Me and the boys, General, sir, we know some of the Indian trails used to cross the Berkshires," Gill tried to reassure Washington.

"I give up trying to play Devil's advocate with you two," Washington said, hands raised in the air.

Knox replied, "I'll take this one map, sir, if you please."

"Yes, of course, and take as many men as you need for the job, Henry. You will be my representative in Ticonderoga. I will give your orders in writing so there is no quibbling at the fort—that you are in charge of the artillery and that you make all decisions regarding the cannons there."

"That makes good sense, yes. To think, had this war not opened on us, I would likely have never met you, General."

"Yes, and you'd be behind your counter in your bookstore, and I would be behind a hoe in my garden in Virginia! Ha."

Ben saw the concern each man had for the other, the comradely regard they held for one

49

another. He hoped to one day have such a bond with another person. He too thought how the war had brought him and Gill together, and how it had brought him to Mr. Knox and to General Washington.

"Return to me in good health, Henry, and you too, Gill, and bring me those big guns, but I truly will not hold you to presenting them in red ribbon on Christmas Day."

This made Gill and Ben smile, and Knox chuckled at this as well, then said, "I understand, sir."

"Do you, Henry, really?" Washington's tone sounded suddenly menacing. "If I must move against Howe sooner than your return, then I will do so—artillery or not."

Knox, McCleary, and the contingent of New Hampshire men made haste to vacate the camp at Roxbury with the understanding that they would be making their way northwest to Albany, New York where they'd be outfitted. From there they'd make their way to the Berkshires, and from there to Fort Ticonderoga in northern New York. Henry Knox made one stop to say goodbye to his wife, Lucy Whitaker Knox where he and Ben Cross found a huge surprise awaiting them—as Henry's brother, William, a boy the same age as Ben, turned up. He'd made his own escape from Boston and was hiding out at his grandparents' home, The Whitakers.

William and Henry had a grand reunion, and William explained how he had used the distraction caused by Ben and Wilbur to make his own getaway in an entirely different direction. He had not braved the swampland, but rather a series of fences and hedges, and he found his way to his grandparents' home, where Lucy had been staying.

As soon as William Knox learned of the trek ahead of his brother, he insisted on being a part of it. "If Ben here is old enough to do his part for the cause, then so am I," he insisted, and it left no room for argument, despite the protestations of Lucy and the Whitakers.

They only remained at the Whitakers long enough to have a final home-cooked meal before rejoining the New Hampshire men and starting out for the western Massachusetts leg of their three hundred mile journey. As they did so, snow began to fall.

By the time it was nearing midnight, Ben Cross and those he traveled with found themselves in a large, hay-filled stable with chickens perched on rafters staring down at the unusual commotion that had come to their home; horses and cows in stalls showed their own displeasure by whinnying, mooing, and kicking out at their stalls. Trying to sleep in the Springfield barn on a hard straw bed would have been impossible if Ben had not been so exhausted.

As they had left Lucy and the Whitakers, reports reached Knox that a detachment of Red Coats had been sent to the Whitaker home in search of Knox, with the intention of arresting him. They'd left just in time, and any fears of the Red Coats giving chase ended miles back. No one expected the

Red Coats holding Boston to venture this far inland, not since the Battle of Bunker Hill and their defeat there.

While trying to get to sleep, Ben, hunched up on his elbow, asked Gill, "You sure the Red Coats aren't outside right now surrounding us?"

"They know they'd be cut off from Boston if they dared come this far west, Ben."

"How do you reckon they knew Mr. Knox would be at the Whitakers tonight of all nights?"

"Old history; they've been trying to get him to come over to their side from the beginning."

Ben nodded at this. "Yeah, but how did they know to come at exactly the time he goes to say goodbye to his wife?"

Gill nodded, and Ned, overhearing, agreed with Ben. "Does smell fishy, Gill. You reckon that ornery father-in-law of his, Whitaker, sent word to Howe?"

"Whitaker's made no secret he stands with the British, a dyed-in-the-wool Tory." Gill nibbled at his lower lip. "But to turn in your own son-in-law? Hard to say."

Ben looked over at William Knox, who was fast asleep, snoring even. He wondered how William had gotten out of Boston without as much as a scratch. A terrible thought flit through his mind. Could a brother, given the divisions created by war, turn in his own flesh and blood? Ben next wondered aloud, "Who else would do such a thing?"

Gill cleared his throat before replying, "Ben, it could be any peddler Knox has asked to supply horses and harnesses for our trip to Ticonderoga."

"Gill you know what I think?" asked Ned, wiping straw from his shock of yellow hair. "Maybe it was that sweet-looking wife of his, his own Lucy."

Gill's reply was laced with anger at the very thought. "Ned, you got no call to suspect the man's wife. Get that notion outta your head now."

"But Gill...think of it...the fact is clear. Knox is without rank still in our army, and he and his wife both know it, and so do the British."

Word had gotten around the American camp that General Washington was taking military advice from a bookseller and one without rank in the Continental Army, as to date no officer's commission had come from the Congress appointing Knox anything but a citizen. In essence, Ned had a point, that they were all put in charge of a man without rank.

"General Washington has put in a request to make Mr. Knox his field general in charge of artillery," Gill countered. "Heard it myself, and so did Ben, here! Didn't you, Ben?"

"Sure did. Plain as a blue sky."

Not too far away from them, Henry Knox rolled over, also finding it hard to sleep, and overhearing parts of what was being said, he got to his feet and walked out into the night. Ben imagined he had a great deal on his mind, and the last thing he needed was his own men feeling suspicious of his motives.

Ned kept talking like a man wound up, saying, "The British seem to think Knox could be persuaded to their side, if given the right—"

53

"Shut up, Ned!" Gill cut him off. "This talk's over here and now. I trust Knox with my life, and you can too."

Ned frowned and nestled into his straw bed. After a moment, Ben rose and went in search of Mr. Knox. He felt somewhat guilty at distrusting William Knox, and he felt some embarrassment at Mr. Knox's having heard the talk that drove him out of the barn. After a moment, his eyes adjusting to the darkness outside, Ben found Henry Knox off a ways, smoking a pipe under the cool moonlit, star-filled sky. He seemed to be counting stars.

When he heard and then saw Ben's approach, Knox tamped out his pipe, turned to him with a big grin on his face, and said, "Men in the ranks are already speaking bad of their leader, eh, Ben?"

"Oh, no sir. Gill's only defended you, Henry, I mean sir."

"Ben, it's only fair, I reckon, when you realize the lowliest private among them has *some* rank! Without a rank at all, they have to be questioning why they should trust me. I'll have to earn it; would have to earn it even if the Congress had ruled on my rank the last time Washington put in for Major Knox. I don't expect to be commissioned a field general, but maybe before year's end, a rank of major *might* come through."

"William, he says you're to be made a colonel."

"We'll have to wait and see. I'm sure it would make a difference with the men. You had a good look at the camps in back of us, Ben...the disorder, the untrained, unskilled, undisciplined soldiers General Washington's inherited. Just imagine how few of them have ever seen cannon, much less fired one."

"What about you and the other members of The Train?"

"Only a handful stand with us, Ben; most are standing with the British, and why? Because they do have cannons!" He laughed at this, and Ben wondered why he found it funny.

Ben did not know what to say, and he feared anything he might say would sound feeble by any measure. Finally, he said, "The general sure has faith in you, Henry."

Knox smiled it seemed at some memory. "We met, the general and I, while he was inspecting field fortifications around Boston. Washington was impressed and rightly so; he couldn't hide that broad smile and his happiness at what he saw that day of the battlements."

"You were the one in charge even then?" Ben asked, curious.

"No one else had a clue, so I stepped into the breach, so to speak. Anyway, Washington complimented me on the breastworks, and he asked me to accompany him back to his Roxbury headquarters and later I became a frequent visitor to his Harvard headquarters. By this time, we had managed to slip three small 3-pounders past the guards in Boston, so Washington was curious to know where I'd learned to build fortifications so well with so little to work with."

"The Train," replied Ben.

"Yes, that's true but also from books!"

"Books?"

"Military manuals I had in my shop, yes. I managed to get hold of every manual available, and I studied them religiously. Why? How many years have we seen this rift between the colonies and the King coming, Ben?"

"A decade?"

"Maybe more for some of us."

"So you were preparing for it all along."

"Read about every great military commander and campaigns ever waged, I did. Became an expert—if I do say so myself, but an untried expert, until now." Knox paused to stare into Ben's now wide eyes. "Do you know what General Washington said to me when he learned of how I obtained my military know-how?"

Ben scratched his head as if it might help him find an answer to Knox's question, but he could only say, "No, sir."

"He said, 'Henry, do you have any of those books lying about?' to which I informed him they were all in my tent at Roxbury." Knox laughed warmly at the memory of Washington's face. "Aside from Lucy, those 3-pounders, the military manuals have been the only items I have managed to smuggle out of Boston. For a long time, the British trusted me and stood aside for me, believing I was a complete Tory and in favor with Howe."

"You made a good spy *then* for our side, I mean," said Ben.

"You could say so, yes."

"So why haven't you earned a rank in the army? I don't understand that."

"That talk of major is all wrong; General Washington early on requested I be made Colonel of Artillery, but without any artillery to speak of…well the Congress has not found time or seen fit to push my commission through. They do have a few things of pressing importance before them, and I suspect some of the members think of me as a Tory spy, I suppose."

"Then they'd be wrong, right along with Ned in there."

Knox laughed, and Ben realized what a great capacity this man had for cheer and laughter even in the face of such allegations. "If only you were a member of Congress, Ben!"

They said goodnight, and Ben returned to his area of the barn, laid down on his makeshift straw bed, and gratefully found sleep.

CHAPTER FIVE

The following day the contingent of twenty odd soldiers, Knox, William and Ben were up before dawn. Gill, Ned, and the others had the saddled horses ready to go. Ben had awoken to a whispered argument among Knox, Gill, and Ned, with William looking on.

"Going by way of New York don't make no sense," Ned was protesting. "That'll just take us out of our way and slow us down—and what Gill says about the changing weather, that's all true, sir! So I still think—"

Knox cut him off, waving papers overhead. "I have orders, men, to proceed to New York before embarking onward to Ticonderoga and upstate. I have no choice, but you do."

"What kind of choice? We've thrown our lot in with you to get them cannons, not to—"

"Pipe down, Ned!" Gill ordered his friend. "Go on, Mr. Knox."

Henry took in a deep breath of air. "When you all get to Albany, look up General Phillip Schuyler, headquartered there."

"But he won't know us from Adam!" protested Ned.

"You'll have papers on you, signed by Washington himself—our orders, men. They will open doors for you, and besides, General Washington sent a post rider to General Schuyler with details of our mission. Orders to lend any and all aid, assistance, and any men necessary to fulfill our mission."

Ned looked around at all the others standing about and he nodded, saying, "Now that sounds right helpful."

"Glad you approve, Ned," replied Knox, laughing. The other men broke into laughter as well. Look, men it is simple. There're artillery all around the city along with battery installations. I'm to inspect fortifications there, and if they can spare any cannons, well…"

"Then we can wait till fair weather to go tromping off to Ticonderoga," said Gill.

Knox nodded. "As you may know, the British have not dared to take New York like they did Boston. General Washington insists I inspect matters for him there *before* we go traipsing off in dead of winter up north, and no counter argument has dissuaded him."

"So we go ahead to get stores and supplies set to go from Albany," said Gill.

"Yes so that less time is lost. Gill, you're to push on to Albany, where I hope to catch up to you before you move out from there for Ticonderoga."

"More waiting," grumbled Ned under his breath.

"Actually, Ned, you and Gill, you two are not going directly to Albany…at least not yet. I have separate plans for you two."

Ben was still stretching as all the discussion was going on. He'd stepped from the barn to see the gray-blue foothills of the Berkshire Mountains to their west; they'd been invisible at night, and it was as if they had positioned themselves here this morning like an army formation that had snuck up on them, rather than being as stationary earthworks crafted by nature. It was one of Ben's crazy passing thoughts, he decided on the spot.

The bulk of the men started off for Albany, while Ned and Gill, held back. The two of them were pointed in the direction of the mountains rather than the Post Road. "Where're you fellas off to?" Ben asked Gill.

"Orders from Mr. Knox—good orders." Gill and Ned instantly loped off for the foothills and mountains beyond.

"Why're they breaking off from the rest of us?" asked Ben of William and Henry Knox.

"They know those mountains better than anyone," said Henry. "I've asked them to mark a trail through them for the return trip from Ticonderoga with the guns in tow."

"Makes good sense," added William. "Smart."

"No one's to know a word of it, boys," Knox admonished the two of them.

"What's your plans for me?" asked Ben.

"We want you beside us on the trail to New York, Ben. I wouldn't feel at ease with you and Will out of my sight."

"New York it is then. Never been."

"Saddle up then; the horse in the stable beside where you slept is yours, and your saddle's on the wall. He's your responsibility now, Ben. Treat him well."

Ben saw that William, too, had his own horse."

They were soon on the road, when William, who'd been keeping a diary of their adventures, asked, "Do you think we've seen the last of the Red Coats for a while, Henry?"

"The uniformed Red Coats, yes…the other variety, I'm not so sure."

"Other variety?" asked Ben.

"The British wouldn't dare try to enter New York Harbor; the New Yorkers have learned from what happened in Boston, so they've fortified against an invasion. On the other hand, they no doubt have *agents* at work in the city."

"Agents?" asked Ben.

"Spies," replied William. "Spies."

Even by cover of darkness, Ben was amazed at the sheer size and bustle of New York City; it sprawled north, south, and westward. The streets were lined with large homes, shops, commercial ventures, with expansively wide cobblestone streets; in fact, here even the alleyways were wide and busy with delivery trams. Coaches, wagons, and carriages even at this late hour passed one another on the same street *without* having to stop for one another to pass first—such a difference from the narrow streets of Boston's wharves and North End.

Knox wasted no time in getting them to the wharves, where he mysteriously left the boys on the dock, while he boarded *The Finn Hawk,* a majestic sailing vessel and a large whaler that had been pressed into the service of the Continental Congress and the defense of New York Harbor. Ben, on first learning of the Finn Hawk and her new use, had joked, "Will they stave off the British with harpoons?"

"They've outfitted her with cannons, Ben—great big, fat beautiful cannons, but they're needed here as much as in Boston."

Left here on the wharf staring up at the big ship with its tall masts and with her rigging creating a lyrical rhythm that recalled Ben's time working at Gray's shipyard back in Boston. Ben studied the ship's lines, wishing that he could see her in full sail, and when Will asked him what was on his mind, he explained his feelings for the ship. "I always thought one day I'd go out on a whaler...someday."

"Why ever?"

"For the adventure of it all, of course!"

"If we can get cannons to Boston for Washington, Ben, that'll be adventure enough for a lifetime."

"I suppose you're right about that."

William tugged his journal from his leather bag strung over his shoulder. He deftly began to sketch the Finn Hawk. Ben leaned against a post, admiring Will for his gift with pen and ink. On reaching the outskirts of the city, an officer had met with them and immediately assigned two guards to guide them to the Finn Hawk. Waiting on the wharf, Will began sketching the uniformed New York militiamen as well. Ben was impressed with the speed with which Will worked to get a basic outline of the ship and the two guards, planning to fill in details from memory at a later time.

Meanwhile, Ben marveled at the harbor lights and the magical city, overwhelming in its size and population. Lost in a reverie, imagining one day telling his children about New York, he paid no attention to the growing crowd of ordinary looking citizens gathering at the end of the wharf. By the time Ben and William did notice the gathered men, another contingent showed up at the other end of the wharf. They began a slow encroachment toward the boys, the two guides, and the ship.

"What's going on, Will?" Ben asked, and Will looked up from his sketch work to see the brewing trouble before them.

Just then the captain of the ship, Henry Knox, and two other officers of the Continental Congress emerged from the captain's quarters when a tall man, the leader of the mob, a large black mustache covering his mouth, shouted, "Colonel Knox is the object we seek; no one else need be harmed."

All of the intruders held single-shot pistols on the men on board ship, and they had taken the weapons of the two guards. Black Mustache added, "No need for you or your men, Captain Blaylock to interfere. We just want the colonel."

Ben saw only one way out. He grabbed Will's arm and pulled him up the gangplank to the ship, but as he did so, he lifted one of two whale oil lamps and threw it into the crowd of gunmen. Will, taking his cue, grabbed the second whale oil lamp hanging at the end of the gangplank and did likewise on his side. Fire burst out on the wharf, sending everyone scurrying, and it gave Captain Blaylock, his armed sailors, Knox, and the other officers a moment to whip out their guns and begin firing at the would-be kidnappers, who were surely British agents in disguise.

The chaos created by Ben and Will had the desired effect, as Black Mustache and his crew raced away below a hail of gunfire. The fiery oil that burned now on the wharf was quickly extinguished by the sailors and the two disarmed guards who looked to make up for their having been taken by surprise. The wooden docks sent flames skyward. Shot were fired on both sides through the flames, as the British agents attempted more mischief from afar, but since the men on board the Finn Hawk had held the high ground and soon dispersed the shooters completely.

Colonel Knox, however, did not feel safe sitting at harbor here. With Ben and Will now on board, he asked Captain Ashabel Blaylock if they could not set sail immediately to avoid another run in with Black Mustache—whoever the agent was.

Blaylock needed no second telling. "We'll follow your plan then, *Colonel* Knox." The captain shouted for his men to set sail for the inlet and the Hudson River, and the old whaler began to creak with movement as the crew went to work.

"We can put the New York officers off at a safe location upriver then," Knox said to the captain and the two officers—strangers to Ben and Will. Knox had been saying to them, before the gunfire, that they had done a superb job of fortifying the harbor. Ben wondered if Henry still believed this after the incident with Black Mustache, but apparently he did, seeing no connection between the two facts.

Once under sail and moving away from the harbor, crowded with ships far better equipped for war than the Hawk, Henry took Ben and Will aside to thank them for their quick thinking and action with the oil lamps. "You boys saved me outright! I imagine, had they taken me, I'd be spending the rest of the war in a prison cell or a firing squad."

The ship moved beneath them in the evening breeze, and to Ben it felt like a dragon awakened from sleep. Feeling her boards vibrating beneath his feet, Ben felt right at home, but Will was feeling the onslaught of sea-sickness as he'd never been on board a ship before. Ben advised him to stare at the horizon, and this helped him some. Beside them, Knox struck up a conversation with Captain Blaylock.

"Your men appear to be armed with crude pistols and knives, Captain. No one has seen fit to arm them properly?"

Blaylock, a tall, spindly and bearded man with a face that looked like a single scar with the use of only one good eye, carried himself with great dignity as he moved about his whaler. "My men are sailors, Knox, used to firing harpoons and spears, but sailors nonetheless, so yeah, they can fight and will fight if and when the time calls for it—as you saw behind us. For them, this ship is a citadel and they will defend it—and me—against all comers."

"I can see you've been in a few battles, Captain."

"I've been to war, yes, and I've fought alongside brave men and cowards alike."

"You fought in the French and Indian War then? Like my father?"

Ben perked up his ears. He knew that Will was proud of his father's having served in that long ago war, but the elder Knox did not return home from it either.

Blaylock took a moment to reply to Knox. "I was in a British regiment then," he admitted.

"So were a lot of men; my father's regiment was a Colonial one, but we were all on the same side then, now weren't we?"

"It's a sad day we've all come to," replied Blaylock. "New alliances, new enemies."

In the distance behind them, Ben saw that the burning wharves they had sailed away from had reignited and burned anew like a crucible in the night.

CHAPTER SIX

A few days later, they put into port at Albany, New York; by this time, Ben had gotten to know Captain Blaylock of the Finn Hawk quite well. The captain admired Ben's skills and abilities on board his ship and offered him a job at sea whenever "This *confounded war* is over, my young friend!"

It was a prize Ben had dreamed of—to put out to sea on a Whaler. The experience and the adventure of it proved powerfully alluring for any boy raised in Boston.

As they entered the port here, Ben marveled at the size of Albany for a city so far inland and away from the coast. William was taken with the place as well; he'd snatched out his charcoal and pad to sketch the docks and warehouses facing the great Hudson River. Henry Knox had taken up a position at the bow, staring hard for someone he thought surely would be on hand to greet them, but so far that did not look to be the case.

The wharves were cluttered with merchants, many wheeling about goods in pushcarts and small wagons along the busy alleyways. A farmer's market appeared to be in full swing below a bright morning sun, lighting all but the densest of shadows, while leaving a nip of cold in the air. A near musical noise of vendors calling out their wares filled the air as well. Now the Finn Hawk sailors began waving their stocking caps and shouting to people ashore. Some called out to the few women that came into their view, calling them Betty and Nanny—making up names as they wished. "How're ya, my darling?" one sailor called out.

"Wouldn't you like to know!" the lady called back, waving a stalk of corn at the incoming ship.

Meanwhile, workmen and carpenters banged away with hammers, building new facilities or adding onto existing ones. The place was a beehive of activity what with the sound of ship building and sawing of wood, and hammering of nails, as well as the braying of mules, the whinnying of horses, and the snorting of oxen. Amid this noise, people haggled loudly over weights, measurements, and prices; they haggled over tea, tobacco, sugar, wheat, barley, fruit, and other produce. It all reminded Ben of how Boston used to look and sound like before the Red Coats had shut down all commerce with their presence. It was as if the war had not come to Albany, except that General Schuyler and his men had been stationed here, and now Henry Knox and his men had shown up.

"Incredible city," Knox said to William and Ben, and he had the look of an amazed man. "Have heard it was thriving but had no idea it was like this and so crowded."

"Bigger'n I woulda thought," added Ben.

Even as he kept sketching, William replied, "It'll be as big as New York City someday maybe."

"Not sure I would go that far," said Henry. "But it is a capitol place."

The Finn Hawk, meanwhile, had eased into the dock like a huge sea creature filled with grace, strength, and pride. Her sailors now worked to secure the ship to the dock, throwing out lines to men who'd already jumped ashore and who caught the lines and secured them to the elephant foot moorings on the wharf. As the ship was docking, Ben watched Captain Blaylock as he shouted orders from beside the wheel. Once the ship was still and hugging the wharf, the captain called down to his special passengers, wishing them well, and then he added, "Remember, Ben. We set sail back for New York, so if you're done with playing at being an army brat for the colonel here, you come back with us. Soon as the blockade is down, the Hawk's going a-whaling!"

William and Henry stared at Ben, who shrugged, and said, "I only told him I'd look him up *after* the war was over with, not before."

"Good, good," began Knox, "because I had arranged to induct you two young men into my outfit here officially, so you can draw pay like any other soldier."

"Really?" asked Ben and William in unison.

"Really."

"We can arrange it right here in Albany. General Schuyler has said so."

"That's grand."

"You two would be drafted in a few months anyhow, and we need all the help we can get on this trip. By the time we're back in Boston, you'll both be soldiers."

As they walked together down the wharf, they found that main street awaited them on the other side of the warehouses. Arriving there, they were greeted by mounted soldiers in uniform, one of them calling out, "Colonel Knox! Welcome to Albany, sir." The man was a dashing soldier with a colorful uniform and he introduced himself as Major John Pritchett. He climbed from his horse and saluted Henry, "So nice to meet you, sir," he added. "We've been sent to escort you to the general's quarters. He is expecting you."

"Have you seen anything of my men in town?"

"Those buckskin soldiers of yours, yes. Who could miss them?"

"I hope they've caused no disturbance."

"No…not at all. Colorful lot, however."

"Have you been in Albany long, Major Pritchett?" asked Henry, surprised.

"Oh not long; reassigned recently to do what I can for General Schuyler. The fellow's up there in years, you know."

"I see. Reassigned from where?"

"Cambridge, actually…very near where you fellows hail from."

"*Ahhh*…then General Washington would have reassigned you here?"

"Yes…yes, Washington." Pritchett's voice gave way to a bit of venom.

"Do you resent the reassignment?"

"A soldier follows orders, Colonel."

"How did you know that my commission had come through as colonel?"

"Oh, it's all the news here—even in the local paper."

"Really? I am flattered."

70

"General Schuyler got word from Washington's camp, and he had it printed as news."

"I learned of it while visiting New York."

"Yes, New York...some troubling business there, I understand."

"We had a run-in with some British agents, but we managed." Henry then introduced his brother to the major, followed by Ben's introduction. Will and Ben both saluted the major in unison.

"We're going to induct these two young men into this man's army while we're here," Henry informed the major.

The major looked them up and down. "I see before me two sturdy soldiers, yes, indeed."

While the major's tone and manner appeared perfectly normal, there was something about the man's demeanor that made Ben uneasy; he struggled with himself to know what it was that intuitively made Ben dislike the man. Was it merely the thick, black mustache which reminded him of the man they had encountered on the wharves of New York? No...not the mustache alone but the eyes. He failed to meet anyone's eyes, this Major Pritchett. Not Henry's, not Will's, and not Ben's. Yes, it was this shiftiness of the eyes that made Ben feel somewhat uneasy.

Major Pritchett's way of carrying himself was off-putting as well, as he stood so stiff and straight as a board even when walking. He managed it without the slightest flinch or slouch or awkward movement, as if every step was planned in advance. He wore polish as well—polished buttons, polished shoes, polished buckles, and even a polished saddle

71

to drape his horse. *Too polished*, Ben thought, but then again, perhaps he had been with the buckskin soldiers for so long that he had begun to resent the other more 'polished' soldiers as a result.

The major walked a little way with Colonel Knox, and Ben overheard him say, "You and I are alike in many ways, Colonel. Both of us are ambitious men, for instance. "and both have, it would seem, curried favor with General Washington as well."

"I suppose you could say that," replied Knox.

"In any event, General Schuyler has the honor of conferring your commission upon you personally, to make it official, so I am to escort you to him."

"You have a knack for making a man feel welcome, John," Knox replied. On hearing the tone of Henry's voice, Ben wondered if he really meant this or not.

"We've been sent to protect you, Henry. There're agents abroad in the land hereabouts, just as there are in New York. I am sworn to your safety, sir, so long as you are in Albany."

"How could any agents here know of my arrival in Albany?" Knox countered.

"News of your proposal to Washington…this *Ticonderoga mission*, has leaked out, Henry. Now you and I go back a long way, and I've promised Schuyler that nothing shall befall you while you're here in Albany."

"How did they know I was in New York, John?"

"They have spies everywhere." When Pritchett said this, he gave a glance to Will and Ben.

Suddenly, there was a commotion as two men pushed through the crowded street toward Knox and Pritchett, and the major snatched his pistol out, readying to fire, when Knox knocked his gun away from its intended target—Ned and Gill. The gun went off, the mini-ball sent skyward. The sound frightened horses and people, creating a great disturbance. All of the majors' men whipped out their guns in response, and Ned and Gill raised their weapons while Knox shouted for calm.

"Hold your fire! Every one of ya!" shouted Knox to both sides. "We're all on the same side!"

Ben rushed to Gill McCleary's side, standing with him and Ned. Gill threw an arm over Ben's shoulder in a protective manner. The major's escort lowered their weapons, and the major put his still smoking pistol back in its holster.

Behind Gill and Ned came all of the other men who had followed Knox, many waving their coonskin hats and whooping. The reunion was complete when Knox greeted them all, turned to Pritchett and his entourage, and said, "Major, it appears I have my escort right here. You may take your men back to their barracks. I am sure I can find my way to General Schuyler with the help of my men."

"Marked that trail you wanted, Colonel Knox," Gill said, and Henry immediately shushed him. Then Gill whispered, "Trail is only fit for snowshoe rabbit and red fox, sir."

Knox's men had formed ranks around him, and flanking him, Ben, and Will on all sides, marched them toward General Schuyler's headquarters. Major Pritchett had regained control of his horse and had mounted the mare, as he and his men stared at the rag-tag *cannoneers* as they were being called by the citizenry here. The well-attired major's men seemed unable to make sense of the rough and tumble, unshaven woodsmen.

Ben got the distinct impression that Major John Pritchett did not for one moment care for the way things had transpired. He had his orders, and he was not happy at all at being unable to carry them out.

General Phillip Schuyler, Commander of the Continental Army of the Northeast, studied Colonel Henry Knox almost as long as he studied Knox's orders. A thin and angular man with high cheek bones and a large forehead, Schuyler was just shy of Henry's height, but he was very much the young Knox's elder—his hair a silver grey, his face a mask of wrinkles borne of the French and Indian War. Concern lay over his features like a permanent veil.

"Why is it, Colonel Knox, that you took a circuitous route to Albany, only to arrive via a privateer at the docks?"

"Semi-privateer, sir, as the Finn Hawk has been pressed into service."

"That does not answer my question, sir."

"I had orders to inspect and report on the gun installations at New York. General Washington thought it prudent; suspected New York of having twice the cannon needed there, and if so…well then…"

"Then a torturous trip to and from the northernmost regions of New York would be unnecessary."

"At least until the weather permitted an easier job of it, sir."

"That explains a lot. I understand you met with a near fatal end in New York City."

"Nothing so dramatic as all that, General, but there was indeed an exchange of…of fire, sir."

Knox wondered at the speed with which news traveled from New York to Albany ahead of them, when General Schuyler began ruminating about General Washington. "I know very little of General Washington, except that he is tall beyond reason and the man's fighting record…well while he showed great bravery, or foolhardiness, during the French and Indian conflict, he hardly distinguished himself as a successful commander."

Knox had never heard of Washington referred to in such unflattering terms, and he did not know how to respond to such words.

Schuyler continued after lighting a pipe and puffing away on it. "As for the selection of the man as Commander-in-Chief by our esteemed Congress…well, that is for greater minds than yours or mine to unravel, eh?"

"I found the general to be a man of great comportment and action, sir," Knox defended Washington.

"Comportment. That's much needed in a war." Schuyler laughed at this. "Action yes, comportment,

75

I'm not so sure. As I say, for greater minds than that of soldiers put out to cover outposts on the edge of civilization."

"Sir, I would hardly call Albany the edge of civilization." Knox started to say more, but the general put up a hand to clearly indicate he should say no more, as if he understood where Knox stood on Washington's reputation. "Washington could have sent another man to New York City in your place; you and your men could well have been to Fort Ticonderoga by now had the general done so."

"He trusts me, sir, without reservation."

"That's all well and good; however, as it stands, you'll be lucky to get those cannons you seek to Glens Falls before Mother Nature puts a halt to any further progress. The weather in these parts is treacherous come the deep snows of late winter."

"General Schuyler, the artillery from Fort Ticonderoga will be useless without ammunition, and plenty, of it. The ammo also has to be forged to size, and one of my chief purposes was to convey this important information to those who have a forge."

"*Ahhh*, I see, yes, of course. I can see that Washington places a great deal of faith in you and your party of Vermont men."

"My men are New Hampshire men, sir."

"Oh, yes, of course." Schuyler then offered Knox a brandy, which Knox gladly accepted. After pouring him a glass, the general proposed a toast to the success of the mission…to collapse the guns of Ticonderoga, tie them down, and with oxen and sleds, haul them to Boston in mid-winter. He ended his toast with, "I will, of course, have Major Pritchett arm you with all the resources at our disposal—as meager as they are, Colonel."

"Thank you, sir." Knox raised and drained the last of his brandy. "Your hospitality is much appreciated. I am hopeful we can find locals who can help us with the number of oxen and sleds we'll need, and if not, that we'll be able to pick them up as we go."

"Henry—may I call you Henry?"

"The men call me *Knox the Ox*, sir, so Henry would be a kindness."

Schuyler's gaze lingered on Knox until he saw a smile breaking on Knox's face. "I can't imagine why anyone would call you that, Henry."

Knox broke into laughter over this and patted his stomach. "Likely has to do with this!"

The general laughed now with Henry. Then he asked, "Are you and Major Pritchett old chums?"

"Not exactly, sir. We grew up in the same area of Boston, but he had a different cache of friends than I…and so we seldom socialized."

"You were both in the Train, correct? The local artillery militia together? He's told me as much."

"Yes…and we were something of rivals there, sir."

"I see. I ask only in the hope that you two settle any differences and get along while you are here."

"Has he said anything to lead you to believe there would be trouble, sir?"

"Not exactly, no…but he led me to believe that he knew you well enough that once you got your commission as Colonel, that you would abandon this notion of hauling tons of cannon over the mountainous terrain in dead of winter and likely await the spring thaw."

Henry felt his head and upper torso move back and up with a gasp. "I don't know what Major Pritchett may have surmised about my character, sir, but once I give my word, I carry through on my word—commission or no commission."

"*Hmmmpf!* When I shared the news of your rank, Colonel, being approved by Congress, he suggested it, and I was inclined to agree, until I learned of you stepping off a ship in our harbor today."

"Major Pritchett should know me better by now, sir. For your own peace of mind, I will tell you that I intend to carry out the mission that General Washington has put me on, no matter what. Whatever it takes, I will have those guns in position and pointed toward the British come spring, and *not* going after them in the spring."

Schuyler smiled and nodded appreciatively. "Cambridge will be lost to the British next, if those guns are not in place this spring."

"Then you've studied our situation, sir."

"I have indeed." Schuyler indicated they go to his desk where he had laid out several maps, one atop the other. "Detailed maps of the Upper Hudson Valley, and the region around Fort Ticonderoga, Colonel. Much better than anything you might have on your person."

Knox beamed. "These are wonderful, sir. So helpful."

"Here, too, is a list of contractors here in Albany and Fort George who can provide supplies, and the oxen and sleds you'll need. The sparse number you will find here in Albany will not do. But none of these goods and services come cheaply, Henry."

"Don't worry, sir. I've brought money in anticipation of encountering those less patriotic than we, sir." Henry did not inform the general that he had emptied his own savings for this venture.

The general smiled knowingly at this. "Contractors are businessmen to the core, Henry. Neither soldier nor patriot, and they will bleed you dry of every cent that Washington arranged for you to utilize."

Henry decided to keep the fact that he was using his own private funds to finance this mission, as neither Washington nor Congress had any money to speak of.

"I believe in the larger cause of the Revolution, General, and I believe in the importance of this mission."

"I see that you are fervent, which is good. You will need that fire, Henry. Now, here is another list I've had my aide compile for you—men you can trust not to rob you blind for lodging and food along the way. In fact, most on this list will not take a penny from you, as they are more than just businessmen."

"I cannot thank you enough, General. This is a boon indeed."

"Not at all, Henry, but frankly, I don't for a moment believe that you have any idea the enormity of the task you have carved out for yourself. The miles between Cambridge and Albany are mild by comparison to what lays ahead of you."

"I see from the topographic map, that indeed we have our work cut out for us, sir."

"You may be dismissive, Henry, all you like of the terrain and the brutal weather you are faced with, but mark my word—but distances on a map cause no pain. Real distances in country like this do in spades. The miles between Albany and Ticonderoga are desolate country fit for wolves and wolves alone. There're areas on your journey that not even the Indians will dare cross in winter."

"We have some excellent men in our troop sir, and we must prevail against all odds."

Schuyler let out a long pent up breath of air. "I wish I were a younger man and a private so that I might be with you on this impossible mission, Henry." He then pointed to the scale in miles on the map atop his desk. "A hundred miles in this terrain may as well be a thousand. I can only hope that God and the angels are with you—and not British spies."

"I suspect the angels will be better company than the wolves, sir!"

At this, the general proposed another brandy.

CHAPTER SEVEN

When Henry Knox finally came out of General Schuyler's office, William, Gill, Ned, and Ben were on hand to welcome him back, and the conversation was immediate, as everyone had questions.

"If we could only wait around here in Albany long enough, we could see Major John Pritchett hang himself with his own rope!"

"Did you discuss that major fella with the general?" asked Gill.

"Not really; I listened more than I yammered. Hey, Ned, I'm picking up your language."

"Didn't you tell him how he nearly shot us?" pressed Ned.

"No, I did not go into any specific details about the major."

Ned raised his voice, asking, "Why not?"

"I suspect, Ned, that Major Pritchett's next move will be, no doubt, an attempt to poison the general's mind against me."

"Why would he do that?" Ned persisted with the question on everyone's mind.

They walked together toward the New Hampshire camp on the outskirts of Albany, the moonlight casting their shadows ahead of them. Henry told Ben and the others, "John Pritchett has always felt that he was eating my dust. He wanted this command—to go after the cannons himself. He has not said it outright, but he knows the reward for

81

success will be great. Simply put—he wants me replaced, and to place himself in my stead."

"He wants our mission, you mean…for the glory of it?" asked Ben.

"That's about the gist of it, Ben, gentlemen." Henry's only show of emotion over this was in his eyes. Ben thought he saw smoke coming from them. Otherwise, Henry remained rocklike and resolute. "Pritchett and I go back a long way, and he likely thinks it is not a mission a mere bookseller can accomplish, and then there's the other notion I had."

"What notion is that?" Ben asked, keeping pace.

"I suspect he was sure that when I got my commission as colonel that I would give up on this outlandish Ticonderoga idea of mine and go home to Lucy instead to sit out the war."

Ben piped up with, "Then the major doesn't know squat about Colonel Henry Knox, now does he?"

Gill added, "You wouldn't let a little thing like a colonelship get in the way of a plan! That's for sure."

On the long journey from Albany to Port George—ironically named after the King they fought—Ben Cross examined his reasons for being here, going northward on an arduous trek with the others following Col. Henry Knox. There seemed to be no single, clear reason, but simply a growing sense of worth and pride in hard work and resourcefulness—an old Yankee trait, for the colonists in the New World had always had to rely on themselves and their own ingenuity. Add to this good feeling of independence and bravado the notions of faithful friendship among the men and great respect for their leader, Colonel Knox.

However, now the weather had become their worst obstacle as it had suddenly turned bitterly cold. The winds howled and froze all that they touched, especially exposed skin. The gusts dusted them with stinging, ice-laden snow, feeling all the while like pellets being thrown into a man's face. It burned Ben's cheeks, nostrils, and eyes. The animals didn't fare any better. There seemed a stony stiffness in the air—like a wall had been built that they must push ahead of them. It was a cold, impenetrable wall of Canadian air sweeping down on their caravan.

Ben's gloved hands felt like clumps of clay, and he had trouble holding onto his reins, but he dared not complain, as most of the men were afoot. The men took turns riding in wagons and walking alongside them in order to spell the work horses. The plan was to purchase oxen in Fort George and Glen Falls as oxen required tons of hay and feed. Nor would it make sense to wear out oxen on the trip up to the fort, but rather require them to do the heavy work on the way back.

Ice caked the entire forest and hills with sporadic areas of green still showing through. Some trees still had leaves flapping in the breeze. The whiteness of snow that threatened to break tree limbs from the sheer weight of layers stood in stark contrast to noisy, splashing waterfalls that came in and out of view as they traveled onward.

The beauty of the falls came as a surprise to Ben as they peeked through the otherwise quiet, heavily forested land. The falls looked like silver ribbons in the distance ahead. The whole of it made Ben think about the immeasurable time it had taken to form the many lakes, ponds, and rivers dotting this landscape.

River crossings had to be made at every turn in the path marked days before by Ned and Gill. The waterways were unavoidable, and everyone crossing knew that if these waters were not frozen solid by the time of their return with the cannons, they would be stranded in this wilderness indefinitely. Still, it was the most direct route to the north and the fort, so they struggled on.

Soon the Adirondack Mountain wilderness engulfed them; Ben felt as if the place had swallowed them up in beautiful gloom: their horses and the wagons along with all supplies had all been gulped down. He recalled seeing Chinese paintings of huge landscapes at Henry's bookstore displayed on one wall, and the people in the prints were near impossible to find in the huge countryside that had swallowed them up. This place reminded Ben just how small he was as opposed to the size and depth of nature. When he remarked on it, Gill laughed lightly and said, "Wait till you see the Berkshires!"

To keep their minds off the bitter cold, the men sang old tunes from a time before Ben was even born. They also talked of all manner of concerns, and at one point, Gill explained to Ben how the Adirondack Indians got their name, the name that applied to the surrounding mountain range. "The

Iroquois, who fought against us in the last war, they had no use for the Adirondacks, so they called them just that—Adirondacks, meaning *bark eaters*."

"Bark eaters?"

"It was an insult. The Iroquois thought them such poor hunters that the only thing they could successfully catch were grubs beneath the bark. Said they made soup of the grubs."

"Ugh! Grubs? Grub worm soup? Ugh!"

"That's how an old Indian I knew as a kid explained it to me."

Just after this and seemingly a miraculous thing, word was conveyed from the front of the caravan that they had arrived at Glens Falls—a handful of miles below Port George. Those who had horses dismounted and walked their horses across a bridge so shaky that Ben and his horse, several times, braced for the collapse of the structure. It was a wooden bridge over an enormous gorge, flanked by a great, noisy waterfall.

They'd been on the road and now this path for two long days, and as they entered the sleepy village of Glens Falls, a place that looked as if torn from the pages of a fairytale book, the villagers opened windows and stood in their doorways staring wildly and unapologetically at the sight before them. They had never before seen so many men and animals on an expedition come through their village. No one knew what to make of it.

By Ben's count, it was December 3rd at half-past 2pm that they came into sight of this hamlet of log homes and a large, wooden stockade, which looked out over the blue expanse of Lake George from its southern tip. Despite the grey and chilled day, the fort looked like a castle to Ben and the others—as it meant a warm place to sleep for the night, a place to build a fire, to have a meal, and to dry out their soggy clothing. It mostly meant a place to rest.

"Going to have to rename this place for sure," muttered Gill in Ben's ear.

"Why's that, Gill?"

"Fort George, Port George, it's called on Lake George. Our enemy!"

"Oh…yeah, of course." Ben stared out at the wide grey-blue lake shrouded by low-hanging clouds that looked ready to open up with renewed snowfall. The water stretched beyond sight at its northern reaches. On their first approach, from a distance, the lake had looked like a small finger or swath of ribbon, but from this vantage point, Ben could believe the estimate on the maps he'd seen, that it was easily thirty miles long and several miles across.

Once the commanding officer of Fort George examined Col. Knox's orders, they were all treated like royalty and given ample space in the barracks with bunk-beds and pillows! Every dog-tired one of them fell onto their bunks and slept 'til daylight the next day—all but Knox himself.

According to word that spread among the New Hampshire soldiers, Knox had spent half the night in the fort's dirty little prison, in conversation with a captured British major who had been deemed a spy. The so-called spy was to be marched to Cambridge under heavy guard, where his punishment would be determined by Washington and the Continental Congress. Ned and Gill told Ben now that the spy's name was Major Andre. Many of the New Hampshire men, along with Ned and Gill, wondered aloud at what could've possibly possessed Col. Knox to talk half the night away with this man.

While Ben did not care for the kind of talk going about the barracks about the matter, he, too, wondered why Henry would give a spy the time of day much less most of the night, especially given how exhausted Knox must have been upon arriving at the fort. Ben had heard most of the scuttlebutt as he roused from sleep. He felt the sunlight of a nearby window bathing him, and he squinted on, looking into the light. Sunlight seemed to have filled every inch of the barracks; every man following Knox was awash in light. A quick glance outside, via a door, had Ben realizing that despite the beautiful bright blue sky, the air remained cold. Hearing complaints of others to close the door, he did so, then returned to his bunk, got dressed, and said, "I'm starved! Where do we find breakfast?"

William, who had taken the bunk above his, agreed. "Yeah, let's go scrounge up some vittles."

"You know, Will," said Ben, "we're losing our Boston vocabulary to Ned and Gill talk!"

"I suspect you're right. I do detect a blending of the two."

After breakfast of hard-tack and beans, they found Ned, Gill, and Effram at the wharf, all staring at Col. Knox who was halfway down the dock and bartering with some boatmen. Ben stared at the oddly shaped, shallow-bottomed craft that passed as ferries here. They were rafts but the French owners of the boats called them something Ben could not pronounce. Ben, knowing a good deal about things that floated, was called to Knox's side for advice. Knox asked him, "What do you think of this type of raft, Ben, for our need to float the cannon from Ticonderoga as far as possible?"

"I...I don't know, sir."

"Please examine one of the flat boats, and let me know if it will take the weight of a two to three hundred pounds."

"We're talking tons, sir."

"Well?" he asked. "Do you need to see one of the boats hoisted up to examine it top to bottom?"

"I can manage, sir."

Ben went to work examining one of the rafts as they all appeared identical. While crude and indelicate, the French raft-boats appeared to be just what Henry Knox needed. "I think you could float a herd of oxen on these things," Ben assured Knox. After fifteen minutes more, he added. "Sir, these are *sound* ferries and should serve you well."

"Excellent! When I saw them from the fort, I thought we should purchase their use."

Ben saw that from a distance, perched on a rise, William was sketching the scene, possibly the ferries, the French owners, Knox, and perhaps even Ben himself.

"You know, Ben," began Knox as he stared out over the expansive lake, "this water here represents our first major obstacle on our return trip, and it will freeze over quite soon, making it impassable, but if we can get the guns to this point via these Frenchy boats, it will be a great achievement."

Knox called out to Gill to come join them, as Gill understood some French, and Knox did not wish to pay a higher price for the use of the boats and the boatmen's time than necessary. The money from his own account was dwindling, and there would be no more. The bartering was quickly underway and not going well when Knox interrupted Gill and said, "Ask them before we came, how much money they would expect to make on the lake with their boats? Then tell them that this is the only offer—no higher!"

Gill roughly translated, and the boatmen huddled together, and discussing it loudly, returned to Knox and Gill, accepting the offer. Before another hour had elapsed, Col. Knox had everyone going to Fort Ticonderoga on the flatbeds of eight pontoon-styled rafts. The only soldiers remaining behind were those left in charge of the horses and the supplies; these men were also asked to locate oxen for when the guns should arrive at Fort George on the rafts.

The raft that Ben and Will were traveling aboard hardly felt to be moving, as the waters were so calm and placid. One of the lakes on the map was called Lake Placid. The Frenchmen at the oars and rudder expertly plied the waters against the current. All seemed to be going well, until Will pointed out one bank, with a buildup of ice along the edge. Next Ben saw large chunks and blocks of ice along the edges of both banks, just lazily floating by, telling a large tale of woe on the way.

The further north they went, the greater the ice in size and cluster. "In another week, the lake would be frozen over," Ben told Will.

"Maybe we'll get lucky…maybe."

"Not likely. We only have two weeks, and from all accounts, there are a lot of cannons waiting at Ticonderoga."

"So we'll just roll 'em out of the fort and onto the rafts," replied Will. "Work fast."

"You never much cared to learn about cannons like your big brother, did you, Will?"

"What's that got to do with it?"

"Every cannon we decide to take will have to be dismantled."

"Really? Oh, yes, of course. I suppose if they were on wheels, they'd roll right off the rafts."

"Sure wouldn't do anyone any good thirty feet below the surface. No, we've gotta break the guns down, and make 'em square and flat and tied down tight." Knox sighed heavily at the thought, then added, "Load them onto the boats flat and as secure as we can make them…likely a lot of tying down, and then and only then will we be float our special cargo down to Glens Falls and Lake George."

Will nodded, understanding better now. "And from there, it's horse and ox drawn sleds."

"And we have to pray that the weather is kind to us—a double-edged sword as we need the waterways to freeze solid, and at the same time, we have to work at not getting ourselves froze in the bargain."

They grew quiet, each left alone with his own thoughts over the enormity of the task that lay yet ahead of them.

CHAPTER EIGHT

Ben stood high atop a large, mysterious crate that had been brought on board the flat-bottomed French boat on Col. Knox's orders. While naturally curious about the box he stood on, Ben felt equally curious about the ferry boats trailing them in the distance. Who could it be? Knox had secured only three of the French boats when all the haggling had finally finished, losing several Frenchmen to bad translation, Ben suspected. He wondered if those who had said no to Knox back on the wharf at Fort George had changed their minds and were racing to catch up and collect for their boats like the others here. Ben had been monitoring the boats behind them as Knox had asked, but oddly, like watching the hands of a clock, they didn't seem to be moving at all. He knew they were gliding smoothly over the water, but due to the distance, they appeared at a standstill.

Meanwhile, they were headed due north toward Ticonderoga. The Lake would at some point return to its source and thus become a river, a river that Fort Ticonderoga kept sentry over.

Having worked in Mr. Gray's shipyard, Ben had thought he had seen every kind of boat there was, but he had never seen the like of these lake boats before, so he studied their architecture and their performance in detail. A pole man walked from bow to stern of the flat surface and propelled the boat by pushing it along by way of pole against the lake bottom. The pole must be twelve feet long, Ben calculated, and the men sturdy enough to urge the boat to go in the general direction hoped for. Another man sat at a tiller, controlling a rudder to help out in maintaining the general direction. The boat's propulsion, while sluggish and slow, made sense on a calm lake so long as the boat was kept to the shallows. The boat was equipped with a simple mast at its center with a single square sail, but without a strong wind, it proved a paltry help in any forward movement. One of the French owners caught Ben studying the boat, and he must have felt compelled to defend it, as he said, "She is swift like a bird when the wind is right, skimming over the water."

Ben continued to have his doubts, but he replied, "I'd like to see that."

"You will...you will."

But so far, Ben had seen no evidence of speed in what he considered a poor man's excuse for a boat. Still as sturdy platforms, Ben fully understood whey Col. Knox wanted as many of these boats as he could rent. The flat bottoms had no keel to get hung up on unseen snags so treacherous to lake boats. They were built to ferry heavy equipment and livestock across the lake. The sides were shallow and without gunwales for easy loading and unloading of men and animals, wagons and now cannons. Still, with their going against the current and with no wind at their backs, Ben wondered how they would ever get to Fort Ticonderoga.

Six hours later, the low-lying stone fort, high atop a pyramidal plateau, showed them her strange outline against the last rays of sunshine on the horizon. Ben and everyone on board the ferry boats watched as the zigzagging shape of the fortress came into focus. It looked to Ben like something out of books about King Arthur and the Knights of the Round Table.

Approaching the castle-like fort from the south by water as they were, Ben first saw the southeast bastion, followed by the southwest bastion coming into view, and that followed by two others in the symmetrical design of the fort. One at each corner. Atop each bastion, men in green buckskin uniforms marched on guard detail—Ethan Allen's now notorious Green Mountain Boys as they proudly called themselves.

Ben tried to make out exactly why there appeared to be a row of what looked like portholes on a ship lining the wall facing the river, but this mystery was solved when Knox shouted, "They've got our cannons pointing right at us, boys!" The portholes were the muzzles of the cannons they'd come for.

All the men moved to one side of the ferry to have a closer look, when the Frenchman in charge shouted in his native tongue that they must not, that they'd scuttle the boat. Both seeing and feeling the boat tipping with their weight, everyone rushed to the other side at once, until Knox started shouting and directing traffic to one side and the other. Ben could now imagine problems loading the artillery onto these boats. It would take some doing to keep the floating platforms level and not lose a cannon or a boat, or both.

Ben pointed out a deep ditch out front of the walls of the fort and asked Henry why it was there. Knox replied, "Notice the wooden lances created from saplings placed in those ditches, crisscrossing spikes. They're quite deadly and difficult to get around. It's just another fortification. The crude lances are half-buried in the ground."

Ben pointed then to what looked like a small fort at the west entryway and asked about it. Knox said, "That is a *demi Lune*—small moon—a first defense against any who attempt to attack at the main entry on the earthen side of the fort."

All across the south entrance along the second story stood a row of barracks, which was repeated on the east and west side, all of it a *wraparound* that looked down on the large parade ground. This common at the center of the fort looked like the heart of the place.

"They have a horrible dungeon in that place," commented the French captain of the flat boat. "It's below ground in a hole blacker than any grave." Ben and Will exchanged a look that asked how the Frenchman could know that—unless he'd been thrown into it at one time. Then again, it could have quite the reputation up and down the waterways here.

The French boatman named Louie, added, "They close a solid oak door over the top of your head! It is *negro*—black!"

No one wanted to ask any questions about this now, and so they neared the Fort Ticonderoga docks in silence. "Is that Lake Champlain coming into view on the other side of the fort?" asked Knox of the Captain Louie.

"Yes, you are right. This is it."

The noise of rushing water over rock had significantly increased, for here the two lakes merged and did battle with one another—Lake George's northernmost terminus with Lake Champlain's southernmost terminus. The two lakes raged as they tumbled into one another. Gill said to Ben, "Indian name, Ticonderoga. It means *Land-of-fighting-waters!* Like a brawl—rapids ahead, but we don't go that *fur*."

Far, Ben wanted to correct Gill but thought better of it. The rapids ahead of them need not be braved, nor did they have to portage, to Ben great relief. They could dock this side of the fort at the elaborate wharves here. They had reached their destination.

Captain Louie, chewing on tobacco, spit into the lake as he and his two men worked to tie up at the docks. Behind them the other boats, six of them now, were doing battle for space at the docks when the little captain said in his broken English to Knox, "Everything that moves in this place moves by boat...by water—or it doesn't move at all."

"We're very near to Canada here, Ben," Knox said to him as the docking completed, and they stepped onto the wharf where, oddly enough, no one was rushing down from the fort to meet them. Knox pointed to the north and said to Ben and Will, "This whole valley's been fought over by the French and

British for nearly three generations, boys, and both countries claim the lakes as theirs."

"Must be important, this place," replied Will, taking in the vistas.

"The lakes here form the most important waterway connecting New York and Canada. Hudson to Lake George, Lake George to here."

The boat captain, hearing this, pounded his chest and proudly added, "*Qui-qui*, the French built the fort in 1755!"

"The French, really?" asked Ben, repeating the *we-we* in his mind as a sign of French pride.

"It was called Fort Carillon then, of course!" replied the captain, smiling widely.

Knox added, "And as long as they held it, they controlled the waterways here. But fortunes of war changed all that. Now it has belonged to three nations if you count America's control of it now! The British had their turn."

"If the fort was taken by Ethan Allen's men without a shot fired, sir, what happened to all the British soldiers garrisoned here?" asked Ben.

"Marched to the Canadian border and told to never come back," Knox replied with a chuckle.

Looking up at the fort now, the walls so near, Knox said, "Ethan Allen must have known how important and strategic this fort was to have acted on his own—well with the help of Colonel Benedict Arnold, whose men were perched and waiting at the entrance. Just a wonder that, without firing a shot, Allen reportedly…singlehandedly took it off the hands of the British."

"Colonel Allen always knows why he's doing what he's doing," said Gill, smiling and adding, "Same as you, Colonel Knox. Don't know about this Arnold fellow, but I hear he's smarting because he got no credit in taking the fort."

Knox nodded at the compliment, gave little thought to the gossip about Benedict Arnold, and said, "Old fort's fallen three times, but don't let that fool you men, because it has been defended successfully too at times. For us, it will prove an impenetrable wall against any invasion by the British from Canada. After all, it was built as a siege garrison."

"So how did Colonel Allen take it so easily?" Ben curiously asked.

"The leadership and the soldiers had grown lax, shirking discipline and military order, obviously without a clue that any American force was interested the place or in the area—and if so, they'd have come by river, giving the British ample time to man their guns. Allen caught the British napping, and he infiltrated the fort by having his men scale the rocky slopes there, a direction no British soldier thought possible to scale."

"They didn't figure on men who're part mountain goat," added Ned, who then broke out in a laugh that wafted up to the guards in green at the fort, who now waved their coonskin hats at the visitors on the wharf.

As they made their way from the docks and up to the fort itself, Ben thought the fort looked like a giant's wedding cake, layered as it was. A huge rail fence helped in their ascent, and all around them the cypress and pine forests were painted with snowfall of a purple hue as the heavy white blanket refused to leave from sight even with nightfall.

The stone slate steps they climbed to the summit of the hill zigzagged sharply, so much so that Ben's knees had to lift so high that they nearly touched his chest. Some of the men on duty met them halfway down these stairs, and Ned and Gill recognized them as brothers in arms. Ben could see why. Ethan Allen's men wore hunting shirts and buckskin coats dyed green, which allowed them to become part of the forest when hunting—camouflage. Like Ned and Gill, they had the ever-present bullet pouch slung over their shoulders, and they carried large hunting knives and tomahawks on their belts. Their feet were covered by moccasins. They were indeed stealthy fighters.

"Why if it ain't Gill McCleary!" declared one of the Green Mountain Boys. "Whatever brings you here— to the last place God created?"

"Haven't you had word up here?" shouted Gill in return. "We've come all the way from Boston to fetch whatever cannons you can spare."

"For a proper fight!" added Ned.

"Why it's old Ned Bottomly!" shouted another of Allen's men.

Knox held up a paper and silenced them all, shouting, "I am Col. Henry Knox, and I have orders to report to General Montgomery—orders from General Washington at Boston. I understand Montgomery is in charge here now."

"No, sir…I mean yes, sir," began Gill's friend, "but General Montgomery's not yet arrived, so Colonel Allen's still headmaster at this school."

"Well then, take me to Colonel Allen, soldier."

"I would but I can't."

"Why not, soldier?"

"He's on a boat on Lake Champlain."

"Doing what?" pressed Knox.

"He's equipped a boat with cannon, and he's…well…patrolling the lake going toward Canada."

"Does he mean to invade Canada?"

"Only if he's provoked to do so, sir."

"When is he expected back? There's no seeing anything in this pitch darkness, no moon, no stars."

"I suspect he's on his way back, sir."

"The moment he's back, announce my need to see him, and see to it that the interview happens tonight."

"Meanwhile, we have some squirrel stew leftovers, sir, and you and your men can find lodging in one of the empty barracks."

"Thank you, corporal is it?"

"Sergeant, sir."

"Good man. Can you see to it that crate the boatmen placed on the wharf gets to Colonel Allen's quarters. It's a gift to him from Washington."

"Yes, sir; of course, sir!"

"Hauled that thing all the way from Albany," muttered Gill, as curious as all the others of its contents.

By now, the Knox party, which included Ben, found themselves surrounded by long-bearded, tall, burly men, all decked out in green buckskin. The sergeant introduced himself as Sergeant Abel Porter, an obvious friend to Ned and Gill. They were all startled by a booming voice from the parapet overhead, making everyone look up as the man there called out, "Welcome, General Montgomery, at last!"

Ben looked up to see a tall, imposing figure there, hands on hips, stance like that of a buccaneer Ben had seen in a book once. This fellow had sandy hair and was waving them on with a coonskin hat in hand. A big man with broad shoulders, muscular arms, and trim waist, Col. Ethan Allen made for quite a sight, but everyone was wondering where he had come from.

"He's done scaled that rock face again just for fun," Porter commented, shaking his head. "And in this wind, too."

Ben wondered if, while on the boat he had outfitted with a cannon, the colonel had been drinking while out patrolling the area for hostile Brits, the Canadians, and Indians.

As they neared Col. Allen, Knox apologized for not being Montgomery, adding, "I'm sure the general is on his way, but we are here to both inspect your artillery inventory, and to collect artillery for General George Washington who is in sore need of artillery at Boston. It is imperative, sir, that we transport as many artillery pieces as we can, as soon as we can."

Allen's handsome face fell as a look of shock came over him. "This is the first I've heard anyone's coming for Fort Ti's guns. I sent word that we plan to march are out of here before deep winter sets in, so if we're to maintain control of the fort, then they'd better send permanent residents."

"Yes, garrison soldiers, I understand. Montgomery's regiment. Must have been slowed down."

"Colonel Knox, your orders notwithstanding, Montgomery's not going to like this a bit, I'm sure, and my advice, if Washington and the Continental Congress wish to maintain control of this area, the guns of Ticonderoga need to remain here—pointed at that lake down there."

Knox took in a deep breath of the cold night air. "We need to talk, sir. If you will approve the bivouacking of my men, I'll share my orders with you in private, and we can go from there."

Allen looked Henry up and down. "Smart to send a big fellow like you to talk sense into me, Colonel Knox. All right, come with me." As they went to Allen's quarters, Ben heard Col. Allen say, "Getting to be too many colonels in one spot."

"What do you mean?" asked Knox.

"Still on the water out there," he replied, pointing. "Colonel Benedict Arnold. Outfitted a boat with a small cannon. It's what gave me the notion, but for me it was sport, to kill time. I fear for him it's far more of a desire to make his mark."

"I see, an ambitious soldier." Knox knew he might say the same of Allen.

Allen laughed lightly now, Knox seeing him recalling Arnold at some point in their history together. "I came on back when darkness began to fall, but Arnold seems to want to kill some enemy—even if it's a black bear."

"I see."

"Do you now? Unless you know Colonel Arnold, sir, you've never known an exhausting man!"

"I do not know Colonel Arnold, no."

"He wants to claim half my plan to attack Canada."

This stopped Knox in his tracks. "You have a plan to invade Canada?"

"Not approved yet by the confounded slow elephant we call a congress, but yes, I do…and now Benedict Arnold is claiming that he had a hand in the idea."

"I'm not so sure it's a good idea when we have the fort firmly in hand, Colonel."

"Maybe you're right, but my men are not the kind of men to be manning a fort; the powers that be need to send soldiers who are used to going nowhere. That's not us."

"I can assure you that General Montgomery will bring men with him to man the fort."

"He'd better for sure; else it *will be* abandoned."

Knox liked the man for his bluntness and straightforwardness, but he wondered if Ethan Allen would not one day wind up arrested and locked up to await a military tribunal. The man obviously made his own rules and applied them in his own time.

Once inside and away from prying ears, the two colonels sat down to have Cognac, courtesy of the abandoned stores of the British officers. The liquid warmed Knox from the inside out. Their discussion on why Henry was here, was brief and to the point, but it also interrupted when a knock at the door was followed by Sergeant Porter peeking in and asking where he should put the crate that Knox had brought upriver with him.

"What the deuce is it, Sergeant?" Allen was abrupt.

"It's a gift, sir," Knox replied for Porter. "From General Washington by way of thanks to you and your men."

"By gosh, it best be filled with rum!"

"Aye, sir," added Porter, beaming with the thought.

"Don't let your hopes soar so high as to be dashed so badly," Knox cautioned them.

"Well open her up, Sergeant. Get some crowbars on it."

Porter and two other of Allen's men carried it in and began ripping the crate apart. When they got the lid off, they found it was stuffed full with uniforms, clothing, gloves, scarves, and long john underwear. Enough for all of Allen's men and then some.

"Washington knows how cold it gets up here at times," Knox calmly said, seeing the disappointment in their eyes.

"Well...thoughtful of him...quite," muttered Ethan Allen.

The men present began selecting their first choices on leggings, scarves, hunting shirts, and coats. "There are two more crates like it on their way," Knox added. "And one with flour and bacon."

"Not one with liquor?" asked Allen to which his men laughed.

"Sorry, no spirits, but there is tea and coffee, yes," replied Knox.

Allen told his men to take the crate out to the common and let the men have at it, with the proviso stating *no fights* and that additional supplies and stores were on the way. Once alone again, Col. Allen asked to see Henry's orders once again. Allen read the orders in silence, and then he said, "You've come to take half or more of the artillery from here, Colonel." He sighed heavily. "I don't envy you your duty or the journey ahead of you, dragging those iron monsters through the wilderness over three hundred miles of rocky roads, Indian footpaths, and places without a so much as a cow path."

"We're prepared to cut down trees out ahead of us if and when necessary."

Allen smiled at this. "I believe you will have to!" Allen raised his glass to salute the success of the mad mission.

"They also said Ticonderoga could not be taken by American forces," countered Knox, lifting his glass, thumping it against Allen's, completing the toast.

CHAPTER NINE

The following morning, Know met again with Allen, and they got right to business on the matter of the artillery, Knox saying, "Thanks for the complete list of cannons, Colonel, but you might start with telling me how many of the big guns are *not* present!"

"Oh…so you've heard how we loaded a few on boats and took them north along the Champlain."

"I did, yes."

"Well fact is, I kind of fear if Benedict Arnold or I had fired off one of those little 3-pounders on board those flatboats, the cannon would've kicked so hard the whole of it would've gone under. So we're dropping that idea."

"Good idea to drop, Colonel, yes."

Allen shrugged. "Only used the small one called a howitzer. Gave the men something to do, rigging them on the boats. Playing pirates, I guess you might say." Allen laughed at this.

"Are the British showing any signs of threatening from the north? It would be foolish, sir, to invade Canadian Territory while our two governments are engaged in sensitive negotiations."

"Don't worry; as long as they stay on their side, we'll stay on our side of the St. Lawrence River, Colonel."

A knock on the door interrupted them. It was Gill, carrying a stack of neatly folded clothing.

"Sergeant Porter, sir, said these were just about right for your size, Colonel Allen, sir."

"Gill McCleary! I heard you and your men were behind this expedition. How've you been?"

"Good, sir, good, and sir, we have every confidence in Colonel Knox here to get this mission done right, sir."

"I hear tonight we have some corn and venison to burn and eat, Gill, thanks in part to your hunters."

"We got enough for everybody, Colonel, yes sir. Should be a nice bonfire on the parade grounds tonight."

Ben watched Col. Henry Knox's eyes grow wide as he stared down the length of the interior wall of captured Fort Ticonderoga. These walls had history, yes, but they were also lined with a beautiful row of artillery from one end to the other—artillery pieces of every size and shape. Henry dreamily placed a hand atop the barrel of a hefty 6-pounder, and next a 12-pounder. His excitement at finally seeing the guns could not be contained. He seemed like a kid in a candy store, Ben thought.

"Look at all of it, Ben, Will," Knox said, astonished.

The big guns, sorely needed 300 miles away, had sat idle here for six months while in American hands, under American control. It had taken that long to hear of the taking of the fort, to then learn of the cache of artillery, and then to convince Congress not only of their worth but of the need for them at strategic locations, where battles would be fought in

107

the spring. A handful of 12-pounders could easily oversee and control the waterways here. Knox immediately saw the waste before him. "General Washington is going to be very pleased when we get back with these beauties," he muttered as much to himself as anyone nearby.

Col. Allen had remained silent, smiling at Henry's response to the cannons. "You're in love, I see," he now said, laughing after Knox who, despite his weight, flew butterfly fashion from cannon to cannon, marveling at each in turn.

The guns here had gone un-catalogued long enough, and Henry put William to work keeping the record as he ticked off the artillery by name and bore size. "We must send a dispatch to General Washington with a full report. We're far luckier than even I had imagined."

"I understand Washington is holding back 7,000 Red Coats with only three brass 3-pounders," Allen said with a shake of the head. "That's a story in itself!"

The calendar had turned to December 4, 1775, and the Boston Siege action led now by Washington was in its 7th month. How long could Washington hold his Cambridge and Roxbury positions with so little artillery backing up his nerve?

As Ben walked along with the group, studying the silent row of cannons, Ethan Allen punctuated his words with a long-stemmed pipe he carried, a sliver of smoke rising from it. "What little I know about cannons wouldn't fill a thimble, Colonel Knox, but I know a lot of these monsters are not worth the risk of your taking them onto your flat boats, then on ski-mounted skids across frozen waters and through thick forests like the Berkshires, and across Massachusetts. The too heavy ones will cost you time and before long desertions."

Knox seemed to ignore this advice, his attention still riveted to the cache of artillery before them. He took his sweet time with each gun as if not wishing to slight the smallest or overlook the largest among them. He even talked to them as if they understood, saying such things as , "Well now, aren't you a lovely, bully girl?"

"Quite the lady, indeed," said Allen in mockery.

"And you!" Knox said to an unusually squat-shoulder 12-pounder. "Aren't you a buster!"

"There are very few field pieces in the lot, Colonel," continued Allen, shrugging. "Most of them are stationary, garrison pieces. Can you imagine the trouble men would have positioning and re-positioning cannons as massive as these? The wheels alone weigh half a ton."

"You don't exaggerate, sir. I see a lot here have been culled from ships, braced on platforms, no wheels at all," Knox replied. These cannon glided back and forth with the recoil over greased metal tracks. "We'll certainly take the lighter pieces—the howitzers." Knox wanted to ease Col. Allen into his true plans, to take away some sixty or seventy artillery pieces.

Knox's keen eye assessed each gun in turn, finding more in each gun than others might themselves recognize. He knew them all from his study of books on artillery. For him, it was a living encyclopedia of artillery that he looked down on, whereas for all the others present, they were just a row of rusting ugly metal objects. Knox, by comparison, searched down each muzzle to determine any in need of cleaning—or *swabbing out*, as he called it.

Henry had a tailor's tape measure with him, and he often measured the muzzle to be certain of its diameter. William was instructed on each number that Henry felt needed to be with the catalogued gun. Many of the guns were stamped with dates and place of origin as well as total weight. Again William was taking this information down for the report to Washington.

After a while, Ben began taking the measurements of each muzzle that Henry questioned. Soon Ben and Will both realized what an enormous task lay ahead of them, as Knox began to tick of each of the guns he meant to see collapsed, tied with hemp, and loaded onto the French flat boats for transport to Fort George, where they'd all reloaded onto the ox-driven flat sleds for travel overland in the snowy north country.

"Cannons are called out by the weight of the ball they fire, boys," Knox explained to Ben and Will as the new colonel hefted a six-pound cannonball. "This ball is fired from a 6-pounder, those larger stacked there—" he pointed to a pyramid of larger cannonballs—"those are fired from the 12-pounders, see?"

Allen added, "Those 6-pounders alone have a bulk of 1600 pounds!"

Ben instantly understood why Col. Allen was being so negative now. "It'd take a lot of horses to pull that cannon into place then, wouldn't it, sir?"

"Six horses to be exact to pull that onto a battlefield, boys, and if one of those horses is feeling sickly...and for the 12-pounder double everything: 3200 pounds and 12 healthy horses."

Knox continued to ignore such talk, his concentration now on smaller artillery. "These small-bore howitzers and mortars need to be counted, William. We're definitely taking all but a few of them. "Especially the Coehorns as they'll be the easiest and simplest to move."

"Which one's a Coehorn?" asked Will while Ben, too, shook his head.

"Smallest of the mortars," replied Knox.

"Why's it called such a funny name?" asked Ben.

"Named for its Dutch inventor, Ben."

"His name was Coehorn, really?"

"Coehorns to be exact, and to you Baron Menno van Coehorns." Knox laughed after this. He then put his hand on a stubby cylinder of cast iron less than three feet long and sitting atop a huge block of wood, to which it was bolted. "Coehorns," he said as if to himself, "who'd have thought to find Coehorns among the mortars at Fort Ti."

Beside the row of Coehorns, sat a row of typical mortars—like the Coehorns only larger, longer, with more cylinder showing, and bolted to their heavy metal casements rather than the wood casements.

111

"These larger babies, Ben, they're more effective than the Coehorns for sure." After this, Knox moved on with Will following as they together completed the cataloguing of the guns. "We have to calculate the total weight, Will, so we have to count the weight of the casements along with the weight of the guns."

Ben, an eager learner, soon could distinguish field cannon from garrison artillery, and howitzers from mortars simply by each casement style. Field cannon and howitzers had the light weight casements so as to be more easily pulled into place on a battlefield, even while under fire. Garrison pieces had huge, stationary and block-like casements or bottoms with small wheels made of heavy cast iron—like those found on board ships like the Finn Hawk. Mortars by comparison were small enough for two men to carry even while bolted to a flat wood or metal casement. Mortars were also wheel-less.

Knox finally completed his inventory of the fort's entire collection of artillery. Once done, he turned to Ben and Will to explain, "There's a large store of grapeshot here, too, fellows, and we'll be inventorying all the ammunition next—but we'll do that after lunch."

"What's grapeshot?" asked Ben.

"Well now, aside from firing cannonballs, most of these cannon can just as well use grapeshot—a canister filled with all manner of sharp metal objects like nails, for instance, that explodes on impact. Its purpose is to slow down or stop the advancing infantry, while the balls are generally directed at a specific target—say a wall or a fortification."

"Which works best?" asked Ben, curious.

"Cannonballs disable or kill only a few of the enemy unless they hit an ammunition dump, but the grapeshot, now that does a lot of damage at every turn." Knox then took Ben closer and around to the front of one 6-pounder, pointing as he did so. "See those elevation notches, each one a wedge? They raise the barrel to get a trajectory to the ball; otherwise whatever is fired from this muzzle goes forth in a flat line. Grapeshot is for straight ahead firing, while cannonballs are for lobbing."

Ben saw the elevation marks at the base of the cannon. "Are the marks accurate, sir?"

Knox laughed and shook his head. "Not very, no! A man must truly *know* his cannon well to make up the difference. No machine can replace the need for brave men, son."

"Can we go eat now?" asked William, sounding weary and slouching.

But Ben had already asked another question: "Why don't the howitzers and mortars have elevation markings?"

"They don't elevate; they're fixed in position guns, tilted yes, but in one position."

"So they can only fire bombs at a high angle?" Ben asked.

"Now you're catching on. "They're mainly for firing at an enemy in a masked position."

"Masked position, sir?"

"As on the reverse slope of a hill, for example."

"*Ahhh*, I see…or over the wall of a fort like this?"

"Exactly."

"Can we go get some food now, Henry?" pleaded William.

By day's end, Henry Knox had a list of the numbers and sizes of the cannons he wished to relieve Fort Ticonderoga of, and he handed the list to Col. Allen. Allen stared at the list for some time as if he misunderstood, and then he said, "This …this is a tall order, Colonel Knox, very tall. Are you sure this isn't the list you intend *not* to take?"

"I can assure you, sir, this is the number of guns we are taking to Cambridge, Massachusetts."

Allen laughed and snorted. "And here I thought I was a crazy man. Colonel Knox, this amount of tonnage over the country you have to go through— like the Berkshires alone! This, sir, this…well it is sheer bravado bordering on madness to think you can manage it, Colonel Knox—or any man for that matter."

Knox replied, "You have your copy of the list. Any help from your men in assisting us in loading will certainly be appreciated. We will have need of the blacksmith shop, for all the metal bands, and we also need all the strong hemp we can find, but you can be sure this is the list we will be working from."

Knox's list read:

Twenty-one 4-pounders
Fifteen 6-pounders
Eleven 12-pounders
Ten mortars

Ten Howitzers
Total Number of Guns = 73

"Some of the guns need reinforcement with wrought iron," added Knox. "I'm asking for your cooperation *and* for the use of your forge."

"You are a resolute crazy person, Knox. I will give you that."

"In general, the artillery pieces range in length from three-foot howitzers to an eleven-foot 24-pounders, Colonel, meaning each must be disassembled and lashed to their wheels, and transported by boat to Fort George, where they'll no longer be your concern, as from there, we shall manage."

The two men had been taking the evening air, strolling along the corridor where the guns sat silent and patient like sleeping elephants Ben thought when he and Will raced up to Knox, shouting, "Henry! You've got to come with us! You've got to see this!"

"What is it, Will, Ben?"

"Come, come!"

In a moment, the boys had led Knox and Col. Allen to an alcove, where in the darkness, Ben lit a torch to reveal a huge cannon twice the size of the largest 24-pounder at the fort. It'd not earlier been noticed as it was under a giant canvass. Colonel Allen erupted with, "Oh, you've discovered the Old Sow as the boys have named it. We keep it covered against the rain. Henry, you have no use whatsoever for her."

"Why not?" asked Knox, examining the Old Sow as it was called under the torchlight. "She's beautiful, your Old Sow."

"Don't even think of it, Henry! The thing weighs 5,500 pounds!"

"Is she in working order?"

"Yes, but think of the trouble she'd be fording a single river, man!"

"Add her to the list, William," Knox said as his hand moved along the huge barrel. "A 44-pounder. I've never seen one before."

"And you never will again if she winds up at the bottom of Lake George," countered Allen. "Be reasonable, man!"

"She's gotta weigh more than all the others put together," Ben added, eyes wide as he helped Knox unveil her entirely.

"Colonel, I admire your...your grit, determination, and tenacity, but how far do you think you'll get with this much cannon alone!" Ethan Allen slapped the cannon with an open hand. "You've got to be realistic."

"I do know my limitations, Colonel Allen, and taking on your Old Sow here, I am going to ask that your men come under my command long enough to help us get to Albany, whereupon, I will dismiss them and send them back to you."

"*Ohhh*....really?" asked Allen, shaking his head. "You are some kind of book clerk, sir."

"I need your men to begin the dismantling work alongside my men first thing tomorrow. I would like you to give this joint venture your blessings, and to convey your feelings to your men so that I might have the full cooperation of every man."

Allen smiled at this. "You will give my regards then to Washington for Christmas on your planned arrival, sir?"

"I will indeed."

"If you make this trip, dragging the Old Sow here with you, and arrive in Cambridge in time for Christmas, Henry, I will begin to believe in angels."

"Get yourself prepared to believe then, Ethan."

The two laughed and Ben and Will found it infectious and began laughing as well. When the laughter ended, Col. Allen said, "My men will be under your command, Colonel Knox; I am sure they will want to be a part of this mission. It might prove even more historic than taking a British fort without firing a single shot."

CHAPTER TEN

The next several days saw the fort come alive with men at work dismantling the artillery and carefully binding each cannon into a neat square held together by metal bands and as a precaution, strong hemp as well. Ben had stumbled on a large supply of hemp, and this sailing ship rope was perfect for the task at hand. The old abandoned forge was fired up, the storehouses thrown open, and tools were taken down and put to use. Teams of men were created to care for each cannon as if the things were delicate eggs. Some teams were sent out to the nearby forests to fell trees for needed lumber, others to cut the lumber from the trees back at the fort. The noise of wagons, horses, hammers, and saws wafted out over the waterways below.

At the forge, soldiers reinforced damaged or weakened cannons. Others merely needed a good scrubbing from inside out. Those in need of attention were soon returned to the lot of those seventy three selected by Col. Knox to go on the long journey. No one truly believed he would in the end insist on the Old Sow, but Henry kept saying that he would take her as well, to anyone who cared to hear it. For Henry, the 44-pounder had meant love at first sight.

The Sow, along with all the others in working condition, had already been removed from their stations, and all were lined up at the gate that opened onto the steep trail to the lakes. Huge winches, the likes of which Ben had not seen since working in Gray's Shipyard, were put to work to lower the readied cannon—those both dismantled and bound in square units—down the slope to the waiting boats.

Beginning with the barrels, each artillery piece was stripped to its block-like casement. Next, they removed the wheels, the larger ones looking like the steering of a tall ship to Ben's eye, and the dismantled cannon looked rather sad and useless, once turned into so many heaps of iron.

Knox, overseeing things, saw that Ben was troubled and asked if all was well. Ben took in a deep breath and said, "The platforms the men have built for the cannons to be carted about upon, sir, I'm afraid aren't good enough."

"How so? What do you mean? They are six boards across."

"There needs be that six and six more crisscrossing over top of those, sir. That is if you want security and safety, should there be any slippage or over the side, sir, else the whole of the affair, cannon and all, could be lost to one crack in the platform."

"I see. Well now, you are the carpenter." With that Knox halted all work and announced the need as Ben had described it. The workmen visibly sank beneath the weight of this extra work put on them. Knox then shouted, "Each platform will be inspected by my Chief Carpenter here, Ben Cross late of Gray's Shipyard, Boston Harbor. You will abide by his decisions on all matters relating to the

119

durability and requirements of each platform. That's an order!"

Ben was shocked at this. He'd only recently been inducted at Albany, and he was a mere private, but Knox had given him this huge responsibility. "Now," added Knox loudly for all to hear, "Private Cross, is there any other matters regarding the way things are being carried out here?"

When Ben hesitated, Knox shouted at him as he would any soldier shirking his duty, "Speak up, man! Quickly now, yes or no?"

"Well, sir, there is the matter of the quality of the wood being used."

"What concern do you have?"

"The men are using scrap wood found lying about—hardened with age and with no give and take in the fiber at all. Now you take those green trees recently cut, and you make the boards from them, then you have what we call elasticity in the wood, a lot more give when pressure is put on so it's not so easy to cause a rent or a tear or a break, you see."

"I did not know this fact, gentlemen! Do you understand why we all must take orders from young Ben here? I believe he was sent to us for a reason."

"There's one more thing," Ben said firmly, loudly, accepting Knox's accolades now without further blushing or shyness. "The green wood still needs to be doubled up on and crisscrossed."

"So, gentlemen! You hear that from our master carpenter! See that it is carried out for each unit of artillery." Knox smiled down at Ben. "You've again proved your worth, Ben. Well done."

120

Ben answered Knox by stomping in to where the men were cutting old boards yanked down from shelters and storage houses, shouting, "The joints and bottoms should be sealed with pitch to waterproof the carriages as much as possible, to prevent any cannon from sinking straightaway to the bottom should it shift off a boat."

The men who already knew this fact grumbled but said nothing. Ben next added, "And since we're going to so much trouble, we may as well do this right and build up sides around each platform for men to grab hold of for ease of movement, and to help keep the bundles bundled!"

"Sides? Like fences?"

"Yes but more like gunwales on a ship," Ben replied. He then called Will over and asked him to draw a sketch of what he wanted so as to show to the workmen.

Will, as he worked, said, "Each unit will resemble a self-contained square ferry boat."

"That's the idea, yes," replied Ben, watching the sketch come to life.

"When the guns are lowered down the hill, these gunwales here," Ben said, pointing to the sketch, "they can easily be put to good use with the ropes and pulleys. Lowered as easily as cargo being placed on the deck of a ship."

Early the following morning and before sunrise, huge draglines of thick chain rattled up and down the valley, the sound breaking the cold air in a series of snaps that sent loons skyward in all directions. Pulleys and winches, so familiar to Ben, were

121

carefully controlled by teams of men holding firm against the weight of one dismantled cannon after another. They began with the smaller pieces, the howitzers, mortars, and Coehorns, and by noon, they began in on the six pounders, saving the twelve and twenty-four pounders for later as many of these were not yet dismantled or bound.

Still, the unsteady loads, awkward in every way, hemp-lashed, barrels sticking far over the side of the gunwales Ben had insisted upon for each makeshift 'boat', were slowly, painstakingly, and carefully lowered down the treacherous and stone-littered slope to the waiting boats on Lake George. The grinding, squealing winches had held all morning without fail, and with each mortar and howitzer successfully deposited on the deck of the waiting ferry boats, the men sent up a roaring cheer. Once or twice, Ned, Gill, and the Green Mountain soldiers broke into a dance on the wharves by way of celebration.

Knox had determined the weight capacities of each ferry so as to know precisely how much stress he could place on their decks. Men would literally have to ride atop the cannons once the ferry boats were sent down to Fort George. Meanwhile, more and more ice had built up along both sides of the tributary here, portending trouble ahead if they did not get underway soon.

Knox now gathered Ben and Will to his side, along with Gill and Ned. "You take charge of this, Will, my ciphering of the weight capacities for each boat we have against the weight of the cannons.

They must be deployed to each boat exactly as I have on paper, understood? All of you?"

They all nodded and grunted.

"Make no deviations from the figures."

"What about that old 44-pounder?" asked Gill. "It'll take a whole boat itself!"

"Since Colonel Arnold has returned, Colonel Allen's turned his boat over to us for the Sow. It will have its own boat, Gill."

"Treated like royalty, eh?" replied Gill, releasing a laugh.

"You four men I trust to be in charge during my absence."

"Absence?" asked Ned for them all.

"Just until Albany, where if all goes well, I'll have secured the needed sleds and oxen. I can't leave a single detail to chance."

"You can't leave us now, Henry!" protested William. "Not with so much literally hanging in the balance." William pointed to the first of the twelve-pounders dangling awkwardly on its way down the slope.

"I've got to go on ahead, Will, Ben…boys. I have no choice. I have to make prep—"

"But so many of the big guns are still at the forge and in the fort, Colonel," protested Ben. "Anything could happen and if you're not here…well suppose the men go on strike or something?"

"I thought all the guns and all the boats would be floating down together," said Ned. "Safety in numbers."

"Listen, men," countered Knox, "we've lost precious time, and I've been delayed here long enough, so it is necessary for me to be back at Fort George by nightfall this day to secure the means of our transportation overland. The waterways will be frozen within a day or two. That's a certainty. No floating our cannons another mile, which is another certainty."

"But that officer at Fort George was supposed to see to our needs, Colonel," replied Gill.

"The same who wishes our failure, Gill, yes, Pritchett. I can't count on his sudden change of heart or in the kindness of others. No, from here on out, we are not likely to encounter another Ethan Allen."

"That's for sure!" shouted Ned.

Gill nodded at this as did Effram, who said, "You've got that right."

"From here on, I rely only on the men placed in my command by Allen and those of you who volunteered at Cambridge. Each step we take ahead of us must be a sure one, if we are to make Cambridge by New Year's Day."

"I thought our plan was Christmas Day," Ned shouted out.

"Given the calendar, Ned, it does not look like that will be humanly possible, but New Year's Day, now that is a day we can strike for!"

Everyone nodded and agreed that they could have the artillery train in Cambridge by New Year's Day when Knox said, "One more thing. I left room on the first boat for that!" He pointed up the slope to where the huge 44-pounder had been lifted and eased over the side and was slowly being moved toward them.

No one was more surprised by this change of plans than was Ben. Gill suggested they all move off a good ways in the event the Sow might take issue with being moved so unceremoniously. She looked totally without grace in her dismantled form; in fact, she looked like what Ben imagined the dead weight of an elephant might appear on a platform.

"I had to do it, boys. I fear if I leave without her, everyone else would decide it Knox's folly to bring her along, but I intend to prove them all wrong."

They all now saw Col. Allen standing at the highest point overhead alongside the dashing Col. Benedict Arnold. Both men had remained aloof and had not interfered with the progress that Knox had made. Knox tipped his hat to the other two colonels, and they in turn waved and Arnold saluted. Both had orders to hold the fort until Montgomery's arrival, which had not happened. Neither man was particularly happy feeling trapped here with winter taking a tight grip on the entire region.

Knox gave a hug to William, shook hands with Ben, Ned, and Gill. "Gill's in charge of the men, including those volunteers from Allen's band. Ben, you and Will, you are in charge of the guns. You know as much about what needs be done as I do by now, so I leave you all to the task and will see you come evening at Fort George. With that, Knox boarded the boat just behind the Old Sow, and once she was in place, he climbed atop the massive cannon and perched himself there like a big troll.

125

He lifted a book from his pouch, one Ben had asked him about, a book entitled *The Ingenious Gentleman Don Quixote of La Mancha* from which Knox had read passages to Will and him during bedtime. Windmills...chasing windmills," Ben thought now as he watched Knox atop the 44-pounder as the first of the ferry boats floated off below them. A mile away, as the boat moved far more swiftly with the current and little need of the pole man, Ben could still make out Knox's shape atop the big gun.

The work progressed even without Knox's presence, as each man seemed to know his job, and everyone felt the weight of just how important the entire mission was to the war effort. The rest of the cannons, even the big 24-pounders appeared to be coming down swiftly and without incident. All of this gave Ben and Will reason to relax and feel good about their chances of leaving Fort Ti for Fort George in good time and in daylight.

William remained stationed with the boats, directing the men where each flat of artillery must go in order to keep the ferry from being overloaded on one side or the other. He must keep the ferries as evenly matched with weight as possible. Ben was more into directing the artillery, lending a hand in actually placing the heavy guns on deck. The flat-bottomed boats proved more stable than Ben had thought they would, and as a result there was very little concern when one favored this side or that to tilt, as this was soon rectified with the placement of the next cannon. There was no stacking of the cannons, as this was impossible, so soon every boat they had was filling to floor capacity. Like Knox, all the men who meant to return to Fort George where the guns would be unloaded, would be riding atop the cannons, nested in their *arms* so to speak.

As the work progressed, more than one soldier lost his footing on the boats and tumbled into the water. The effect was to fill the air all around Fort Ti with the sound of laughter and cheers by way of thanks for the laughter.

As the line of men and cannon zigzagged along the bluff over Ben's head, he studied how it was a stop and go affair. The cannons stopping and starting like so many stubborn, unwilling animals with trunk-like snouts rather than static metal. The cannon trail followed along a pair of huge chains, and all was going well when one chain snapped, sending one cannon, a 6-pounder, lurching forward and straight at the men below it, sending men scurrying and shouting in all directions. The big gun tipped awkwardly, groaned against the chains and pulleys, and dropped like a square boulder, awkward and ugly as it bounded halfway down the slope without any help other than gravity, until it finally came to rest.

"Good God!" shouted Will.

"Yeah, looked for a moment like it was coming straight for the dock, and if it hit one of the loaded boats, it would've sunk them all for sure!"

"We need to start moving out the boats that are loaded, at least to get them away from the docks." William looked about for Gill, finding him crouching still and staring up at the ruckus above where the 6-pounder had dropped and now dangled awkwardly where it rested. Gill listened to reason and ordered Ned to take two men and get the loaded boats away from any such danger. They were to take them out a hundred yards and wait for the rest to join them, as everyone agreed they should caravan down together.

Ben now said of the cannon that had slipped its moorings, "Let's have a look at the damage; see if she's still worth our time." He and Ned calmly climbed up to where the gun rested. They inspected it, and in a moment, Ben shouted out to everyone, "The platform's intact! Not a crack in her, and the gun's okay too."

Gill added, "Boys, we've gotta be more careful! This can't happen again. Watch the stress on the line. Get the inspectors working overtime."

"We don't want anybody injured!" added Ben.

By early afternoon, all the boats were sitting low in the water under the weight of their cargo, loaded to capacity. Every gun Henry had catalogued to go was on board flat boats. The last man joining them got on board, and the French boatmen expertly tied each raft together, creating one huge monstrous image on the lake for Colonels Arnold and Allen to watch disappear into the distance.

On board the monster cargo *barge* created of the lashed boats and cannons, Ben waved goodbye to the relative safety of Fort Ticonderoga where a man could find a meal of bread and potatoes at very least, a campfire, and warmth. Already the lake was freezing over, and the wisdom of lashing the boats became clearer still as the barge broke the ice before them far more efficiently than a single boat might do. The combined weight of the lashed boats also worked better with the current than the boats would find separately.

They remained in sight of the fort when a blotter of dark clouds began moving across the sky, causing worry among the boatmen in particular. Lake George was a monster-sized lake, and a storm on this lake, Ben was told, could turn frightfully ugly at a moment's notice.

An hour later, the dark grey, revolving churning clouds turned day into *a mid-day night*, and an incredible wind swept over the sails of the barge, forcing the boatmen to pull their sails in for fear of being controlled by the turbulence. The wind began threatening their entire enterprise before it had even begun, Ben feared now. Huge cold pellets of rain lashed out at the men and stung Ben's face no matter what direction he faced. As he turned, Ben noticed that one boat, the first in the line of boats had left its sail up—Ned's boat, and the wind was ripping into the sail and taking them off course.

Ben didn't stop to think. He suddenly began leaping from boat to boat, climbing over the artillery, passing by men who had curled into balls against the storm, but *he* meant to get at that sail. He reached the front boat with only a few bumps and bruises. He shouted at the boatman in charge to drop the sail, but the man was not about to move from the cover of a tarp draped over the cannons as the wind whipped all about them. The barge was being turned awkwardly to the port side and was in danger of being dashed against rocks and snags. To be safe, they must stay on course and maintain a goodly distance from the rocky shore that the wave seemed bent on sending them into.

Ben knew enough about rigging to get the sail down himself, but he now saw that Gill McCleary was with him, and together, they brought the sail down despite the merciless beating both the flapping sail and they themselves were taking from the storm. Ned, like the boatman, had taken shelter below the tarp.

The boatman shouted from below the tarp, "We've only made five nautical miles, but we better put to at Sabbath."

"Sabbath is Sunday," said Ben.

Gill replied, shouting over the storm, "Sabbath is a sandy shore, Ben. Saw it on the maps."

"Oh…oh yeah?" He then asked the boatman, "Is it safe harbor?"

"Yes, but you must tell the captain in the rear…as the last boat now controls them all with the only useful rudder."

The other boats had all been turned with rudder's lifted and lying useless on board. As a barge, there could only be one controlling unit. As it was, the storm threatened to take the barge apart raft by raft. Ben feared if this was to happen, then they could lose some or all of the cannon to the deep.

Again Ben traversed the length of the barge, and with each leap, he felt the shudder of each boat wishing to separate itself from her moorings with the other boats. He finally managed to get to the rear boat after a moment's fear of being blown over the side by one gust. There he informed the French

130

boatman with a single word he would understand: "Sabbath!"

William and Ben now tried desperately to see through the wall of rain when suddenly they did in fact see a handful of smoke stacks. Homes in the wild. Still at the front on deck, Gill was pointing and shouting, "Take her in!"

There was no dock, only shallows of a sandy nature in which to find safe shelter. The boatmen readied their anchors and began tying ropes to trees on either side to secure the barge. They were soon at rest on the huge sandbar called Sabbath Day Point, and while the wind continued to buffet them, here at least, they had some measure of stability and control.

The rear boat was the most exposed to the whipping winds, and it listed to one side, threatening to be pulled away from the others and carried downstream. Just then the boat hit a snag near shore, causing one of the cannons to shift, which had the entire boat teetering for a moment as if it might snap off from its moorings entirely. Fortune held along with the moorings and anchor. Now the waves battered them all. The shifting of the cannon slabs could easily injure a man, and for this reason most remained perched atop the cannon—for the moment, the safest place to be.

Then it happened and everyone heard it. What was thought to be a secure line snapped, causing a 24-pounder to slide over the side and crush the tree trunk below the waterline, which caused the snag in the first place. AS soon as this loose cannon went over the side, the rear boat righted itself and

131

remained safely attached itself as part of the barge. Still, the loss of the single cannon sent a shard of pain through Ben. He felt he'd let Col. Knox down.

Gill, standing alongside him said, "It'll be all right, Ben. It's shallow water, and come morning and daylight, we'll fetch it out and secure her same as before. Well, not *same* as before—*better* to be sure."

"Who could've planned on this weather?" said William, joining them.

"At least no one was injured," added Ned.

All of them were soaked through from the rain. Cold and exhausted, the men found solid ground and began to build fires to warm themselves when a handful of people emerged from the few cabins at Sabbath Day Point and on learning what this party was all about, invited the men inside to dry out and share beef jerky, hard-tack biscuits and gravy.

As they entered the dry, warm cabin, finding a roaring fire in the hearth and the smell of rabbit stew from one pot, Ned said, "Lord, Ben Cross, I thought we were all goners for a minute there! That rope snapped like a ripe ear of corn."

"I told you all to use hemp on every cannon," Ben replied, unhappy.

"We did but we ran out of hemp."

"It's all right, Ben," Gill again reassured him. "It's really no one's fault."

All the same, Ben felt ill, his insides churning at the thought of the lost cannon, its barrel sticking out of the water while the rest was below. "I suppose in another minute or two, the whole raft

132

might've overturned and men could've been injured or…or lost."

"Hardly five miles from the fort," lamented Effram, warming himself by the fire.

"Only two-hundred and ninety five more miles ahead of us, Effram!" shouted Gill in response.

Ned joined in. "If we lose one gun for every five miles, that'd leave us with none for Washington in the end!"

"We've not lost that bruiser out there, Ned. She'll be waiting come sunup. We can raise her."

"We only need right the platform," added Ben, nodding now. "That snag has it now but if we can loosen her up, she'll float."

"Thanks to your design, Ben," added William.

"That's enough feeling sorry for ourselves," said Gill, wishing to put the subject to bed.

"King George's revenge, you might say," replied the burly Effram. "That lake out there is named for him, remember?"

Ben wondered how many of the men were superstitiously inclined. He and the others were exhausted, having spent most of the day loading the cannons, and much of the evening fighting a nasty storm.

It rained for most of the night, and the men who could not be accommodated inside the cabins had somehow managed to pitch tents and were huddled in them for the night. Some found sheds and barns offered them by the few inhabitants of Sabbath Day Point. A bonfire was lit outdoors, and its roaring

133

flames brightened the dreary beach. Finally, the rains slowed and stopped altogether.

The morning stillness and sunshine peeking over the horizon together proved welcome relief, but when Ben looked out at the sad barrel of the errant artillery piece stabbing skyward, half under water, his stomach churned anew. They were supposed to have been in Fort George the previous night at the latest, and now this delay. One side of the boat the cannon had slipped from had taken a terrible pounding as well, visible only now in the light of day.

The delay was compounded as they must unload the rear boat in order to get it to ground for repairs while another crew worked to right the artillery piece and float it ashore. Ben and the others agreed that all the other boats should go on ahead to Fort George rather than sit idle while repairs and reloading of the injured boat were underway. William and Ned were sent ahead with the cargo of cannons, while Ben and Gill remained to oversee the repairs and outfitting of the last boat.

Several hours had passed before the work was done. They'd had to refloat the raft, as they could not budge the stuck raft itself with the weight of the guns on board. This had meant unloading, and later reloading, each artillery piece one by one. The final 24-pounder to be loaded was the one that'd gone over the side, the same one that the men had begun to call the Little Sow. Once this final piece was set in place, Ben leaned against the Little Sow and breathed a sigh of relief. They had lost a day no one could get back, and New Year's Day was coming soon. He puzzled over how the rope that had sent the one cannon into the drink could have been cut by someone in their number, but who would do such a thing? Who would intentionally cut that rope? He'd examined the rope carefully, and he knew the difference between a snapped length of rope and a cut line. He had not shared his knowledge of this with anyone, not even William or Gill, and he wondered how Colonel Knox would take the news that someone in their ranks, or one of the Green Mountain volunteers, or one of the French boatmen, had surely sabotaged their efforts, costing them precious time.

The storm itself had been the perfect cover for sabotage. It had been as underhanded as it gets, Ben thought now. He felt a welling up of guilt from within at having confided this to no one, not even William or Gill. He tried to act as naturally and as calmly as Gill had been throughout the *accident*. Ben also thought of the variety of reasons *why* or *how* a man could be brought to sabotage the artillery train: *patriotism* toward the other side, *revenge* against Knox, a hefty *payment*. "Someone definitely has a reason. That much is for sure," he muttered to himself.

Gill had walked up behind him, and he quietly said in Ben's ear, "If there is a saboteur, Ben, best way to catch him is to pretend we don't know a thing."

Ben wheeled and stared into Gill's smiling eyes. "You know then?"

"I saw the same evidence you did, son."

Ben's relief at having someone to share this heavy burden with washed over him like a welcomed balm. "I can't imagine who, but I suspect the boatman at the rudder did it."

"No proof of that, Ben. We don't want to start looking like a pair of vultures, suspicious of every man who talks different or shirks off a bit on his work day."

"I guess not, but what do we do?"

"We keep our eyes and ears open, close to the ground as they say."

"Whoever he is, he could strike again—at any moment."

"Aye…so we have to stay vigilant, Ben."

"I *have*. I inspected every inch of hemp on all the other boats before they left today, Gill. This deviltry, you know, it started back at the that fort, when mere rope was used on that one cannon instead of hemp. I find it hard to believe we suddenly didn't have enough hemp to use."

Hemp absorbed water and only became tighter as a result, and Gill knew this as well. "I take your point. Someone at Fort Ticonderoga, who came right along with us."

"It could be one of Colonel Allen's men, Gill."

"Could be."

"Or the Frenchies. They were at the fort, sleeping over."

The two looked at one another. "I guess then anyone who was at the fort has to be considered under suspicion," said Gill. "You don't suspect me, do you , Ben?"

"No…no, of course not."

136

"Good because I have no reason to suspect you. What do you say to our shoving off now for Fort George before we lose all daylight?"

"Yes, of course!"

Gill shouted out to the men, "All aboard who's ferrying to Fort George! We're off, lads!"

It was now late afternoon Everything had taken a terrible toll of time and the frigid waters had only become more laden with brittle ice. *Something the saboteur, no doubt, counted upon,* Ben thought as he watched Gill wave the others onto the raft. They would arrive at Fort George while the town and fort slept, hopefully before dawn. The usual half day's boat ride from fort to fort will have taken them two days.

CHAPTER ELEVEN

They arrived at the Fort George stockade just before daybreak. Ben exhausted and weary-eyed, was hardly able to focus on the last of the cannons now fitfully bumping the docks until all lines were secured. But by then, Ben—wrapped in an Indian blanket, had fallen asleep atop the Little Sow. An hour later, he was roused by the large hands of Colonel Knox, and in his ear, Knox said, "I knew I could count on you to get the job done, Ben."

"But we're a day and a half, two days late, Henry...*ahhh* Colonel."

"And how many cannons did you lose, Ben?"

"Why...why *none*, of course, sir!"

"Then you were successful, and I am extremely proud of you."

"Thank you, sir," said Ben, beaming despite his weariness.

"Excellent. Now there's a cook inside with a hot bowl of stew, a hot potato, and a hunk of bread waiting for you. Gill and the others are already inside and chomping down on breakfast."

"Inside where?"

"The warehouse right here; we've confiscated it for our needs. It's also a might bit warmer place to catch some sleep."

"I have a great deal to tell you, Colonel."

"I've heard all about the accident, Ben. Now go get some grub."

"But sir," Ben whispered, "it was no accident. Gill and I both believe it was deliberate sabotage, Colonel."

"What are you saying, Ben?"

"There's a traitor among us, sir." Ben had held onto the length of rope that he'd judged to have been tampered with. "This was cut by a knife, Colonel. It gave way because it was half sliced into, weakening it, and the storm did the rest."

Gill had returned with hot grog for Ben, and Knox asked him if he believed as Ben believed. Gill did not hesitate, saying, "Ben's right; he's got a sharp eye, the boy does."

"It might've been someone at the fort before we shoved off," suggested Ben.

"Might just as well have been tampered with in hopes it would tumble down the hillside," added Gill. "We had another cannon slip and fall as we were loading, but we all took it to be an accident, but now…"

"Now who's to say?" finished Ben. "Then again, it could be someone among us now, here, eating our food, drinking our drink, warming himself by the fire inside…just biding his time to strike again."

"We've had no misfortunes befall us in unloading the boats that came ahead of you, Ben, Gill. Perhaps the misfortunes are behind us." Knox smiled. "You fellows have done a fine job of it."

"I just hope we aren't plagued by evil intentions from here to Cambridge," replied Gill, stating what was on all their minds.

"When do we leave Fort George, sir?" Ben asked.

"We've got everything loaded onto oxen-drawn sleds, all but your cargo here. We do that, and we're on our way—say in an hour's time, maybe two, so go inside, get some nourishment and some sleep near the hearth."

"But what shall we do about the saboteur?" Ben pressed him.

"Best we can do is make a formal check of all cannons and their security before each day's journey," Knox shot back. "It'll slow us down some, of course...but that's likely just what they want—whoever *they* are."

"They? Do you suspect more than one man?"

"Usually these sorts of underhanded matters involve conspirators. Ethan Allen was not exactly pleased that we took as many guns as we did from his fort, and Arnold—that other fellow—was even more put out."

"But they are both colonels in the army," Ben protested the idea.

"You saw how well behaved Pritchett was here in Fort George, and he's a major."

"Yes...I see, but Colonel Allen and Colonel Arnold?"

"Arnold maybe, sir," said Gill, shaking his head, "but Colonel Allen would never be a part of such a thing, never."

"I'm sure you're right, Gill. I'm just thinking out loud is all." Knox led Ben to the warmth of the warehouse. Inside the huge barnlike structure, all the cannons were present and had been loaded onto

140

sleds. In one area, the huge, black oxen stood about in a clump. This was the staging area from which they would launch the long, long journey overland from here to Cambridge while transporting seventy three pieces of field artillery and some pieces Henry hoped to forge into field artillery once they got to Cambridge.

Ben also saw men in various stages of wakefulness, some being roused by Knox to get the final boat unloaded. Among those he saw awakened was Ned Bottomly, who upon seeing that Gill and Ben had arrived, exploded in a war-whoop loud enough to wake the dead. When others saw that the men with the final boat had rejoined them, a huge cheer went up, the sound of it filling the old warehouse and frightening the animals. Even crotchety old Effram was smiling and nodding and appreciatively tipping his hat in exaggerated fashion to Gill, and next to Ben. He looked like a theater actor, taking a bow, Ben thought, the way Effram twirled his hat. All he needed were some plumes to complete the picture. Ned was more subdued, looking tired, but not so tired that he could not poke fun at Effram's antics.

All the while, Knox maintained a profound calm and his wide grin, even knowing what Ben had told him. *The man is like a rock*, Ben thought, wishing he could be more like him.

A groan went up among the men even as Gill McCleary shouted, "You heard Colonel Knox! Every man to work, and put your backs into it."

Some of the soldiers were sitting on rocks, others leaning against trees and walls. When Ben approached, he saw a dispirited bunch indeed. They had already labored for many hours to get the artillery pieces moved from the boats and onto the ox-drawn sleds.

Ben also saw Knox, standing tall and firm, staring out at the frozen lake which had pretty much decided to strand any and all boat traffic for the duration of winter. Still the ice was not thick enough or safe enough to utilize with oxen and sled. The poor things would go straight under, and being harnessed to the sleds and cannon, they'd drown for sure. This meant, as planned, an overland route must be used, at least until which time as the rivers and lakes did become frozen corridors. Then the waterways would help rather than hinder their trek southeast from Upstate New York to Massachusetts. Two hundred and fifty miles was the round number of miles lying ahead of them.

Knox turned from staring out at the frigid waters of Lake George to glare at the little man beside him who wanted more for his oxen team and sleds than Henry wanted to pay. They were haggling over the price, and this only added to the depressed scene that Ben found before him.

"You won't find no other sleds or oxen, Colonel, not hereabouts and not in Glens Falls," shouted the little man with his scraggly beard bobbing as he did so.

"You're a highwayman, sir, and your price has doubled since last we spoke! It won't do." Knox did not shout, but his firm words remained calm and measured.

"Suit yourself, Colonel, but I've come a long way with my team and sleds in tow just for you, sir, so I expect better for my trouble!"

"How about a week in the fort here—locked up and under guard for attempting to rob the Continental Congress, Mr. Farley?"

The man named Farley gasped at the idea. "You can't throw me in jail. I am a private citizen...not part of your army!"

"I am sure General Schuyler would indulge me in this matter, Mr. Farley. Now, we can either agree on the agreed upon price, or I can have you arrested, and we will simply confiscate the needed teams and sleds and be on our way."

"Who's the highwayman now?" asked Farley.

Ben realized that this Mr. Farley had only increased his price *after* the sleds were fully loaded. Only a few artillery pieces remained on board the last boat, the one that Ben had brought in. After so much labor already expended, to have the oxen man balking at the price and threatening to have the sleds returned to him, Ben could well understand why the men had gone into such a bad temper.

"All right," began Farley. "I will accept the price for the sleds as we had agreed, but I want the extra on the animals."

"No deal, Mr. Farley," replied Knox, standing firm. "Corporal McCleary, two men, escort Mr. Farley to the jailhouse at the fort."

Gill quickly called out Ned and Effram for the work, and Mr. Farley decided he would not dare call

Knox's bluff. "All right...all right! But you're going to have to find feed and water for the animals and keep 'em fit. When they're returned to me, they better be in fine fiddle. My sleds, too."

"We will take all due care with your animals and sleds as if they were our own," replied Knox, and the irony of his remarks were not lost on Ben as he watched Farley take his payment and rush off.

"Not one patriotic bone in the man's frame," Knox said to Ben, Gill, and the others, to which the men sent up a laugh.

Just then what seemed to be a handful of large angel feathers drifted down to them, fluffy white snow that seemed like the most benign snow Ben had ever seen; it was that pleasant. The men went back to work, and soon the final piece of artillery was loaded onto the ox-drawn sleds. The shiny ski runners glistened in the sunshine as the pretty snowfall continued, each flake picking up the sunlight that passed through it. One flake came to rest on Ben's nose and he blew at it to see it fly up and away like a butterfly.

"Snow!" shouted Knox, happy at the sight. They all knew that now the more snow, the better for the sleds required snowfall and lots of it.

"You call this snow?" asked Ben, shrugging.

"This is a harbinger of more snow, Ben. The real show will come by noon, I warrant." Knox then shouted to his men, "Our luck's finally taking a turn for the better, men!"

Gill cautioned, "Yeah, but we better pray we don't get caught in a blizzard, Colonel."

"Say goodbye to Fort George!" Knox replied to them all, and the oxen teams began the first step of their long journey.

The snow did not disappoint. What had begun as pleasant, quickly turned to an eruption of the white stuff, covering the ground, the backs of the oxen, the cannons in their canvass beds, the horses, and the men. The soldiers were exhilarated; they were much happier on solid ground and even happier that their mission was finally, and really, underway. It was no longer about back-breaking loading and unloading of heavy machinery, for now it was the trek south for the waiting battlefield at Boston.

All the same, even with the snow and the combined spirit of the men running high, and despite Knox's optimism and grand prediction that the artillery would be in place by New Year's Day, the craggy, difficult paths they ventured into fought each cannon sled for every inch and foot. Already, some sections of the forest had to be cleared ahead of them, so teams of tree cutters could be heard off in the distance for this very reason. Other sections proved impenetrable, forcing them to back-track and seek out another route around this or that area. Words like impassable and zigzagging had become the watchwords the men knew all too well.

The artillery train found itself stopped over and over again. The train itself was a long, twisting snake curling about the forest now. The land threw up enormous bluffs, clefts, trenches, gullies, and gorges that no man could challenge, Knox's

145

scouts—Ned and Gill—must find another way, which usually meant that miles needed to be added to the journey. Usually, it also meant that the train sat idle for hours—waiting for words like *passable* and *this-way*!

Early afternoon brought on a howling wind that sent the falling snow into Ben's face and eyes, stinging like bees. The temperature began dropping rapidly as well as all the men began to feel the cold deep in their bones. Men stumbled over logs and rocks buried beneath the snow, as dead and fallen trees dotted the landscape, and the earth here seemed to produce stones as if they were the natural bumper crop of the wilds. Often the train was held up so that men could remove boulders and take their axes to fallen trees to clear the way forward. With each stop, the cold settled more deeply into Ben's flesh and bones, making his hands so stiff even inside his gloves. This made working the reins to the oxen difficult. He'd spelled another soldier only an hour before, but it felt like an eternity.

The snow eased the load for the oxen, and they worked extremely well along flat stretches, but there were so many hard gradients, drops, falls, and craggy embankments to maneuver on the slopes. Going uphill was terribly hard on the animals, but gliding down the other side, while far easier, also proved perilous, and brakes had to be applied as a result. It meant holding a brake to the point of exhaustion. The sleds were lashed by chains, draglines, block and tackle, and so they must be let out with ease down the steepest of gradients. Chains had to be wrapped about trees and let out slowly and safely. The sleds, on their icy runners, had proven capable of injuring animals and men; the soldiers knew that their burden could kill a man if he found himself in the wrong place at the wrong time. Ben had watched helplessly as the sled ahead of his had escaped, so to speak, and had gone wildly downhill, completely out of control.

It was an 83-sled train that Knox was overseeing. Seventy three sleds held artillery, while the rest carried needed supplies for the long journey—from tents and tools to food and water. Knox had divided the train into three sections, each under the command of his most trusted men, who'd had experience with such travel. One section was put under command of Private Ned Bottomly, the other under Gill McCleary, and the third went to Effram, while Knox oversaw all three sections. By early afternoon, they had only traversed seven miles south of Fort George, when the train was halted by Major Pritchett, acting as courier from General Schuyler.

"Seven miles," Ben groaned and halted his new habit of throwing wood chips onto the backs of the oxen team he drove—an old timer's trick to keep them moving. "We've only come seven miles? It feels like seven hundred."

Knox read the note handed to him by Pritchett, which essentially ordered him and the entire train back to Fort George without any explanation. Amid a great deal of anger and frustration rising up from the men, Colonel Knox quelled them with his own anger. "It is an order from a general in the army in which we serve, gentlemen! We must obey it. Now…turn the train back for the fort."

Knox then asked Pritchett, "What is behind this order, John? I have a right to know."

"Trust me. It is for your own good and the safety of your train." Pritchett refused to say anymore, riding off in the direction of the fort from which he came.

The setback dampened everyone's spirits anew. The struggle to get this far had been a gargantuan one. Still, these were orders signed by the general. There was no refusing them. The mystery as to why still hung over the camp like a pall. When a second rider from Fort George arrived with *counter orders* to push on to Glens Falls. The two conflicting messages confused Knox, but he needed no second telling to push forward rather than back to Lake George and the fort. He muttered to Ben and Will where they sat on a sled seat, "Major Pritchett did say 'trust me' didn't he?"

"Yes, he did," agreed Will.

"Which means don't trust him," added Ben.

"We'd have gotten all the way back to be told it was a miscommunication, no doubt." Knox tore up his one set of orders for the sake of the other, more welcomed news. He then shouted out his order to his men to carry on to Glens Falls.

The order recalled to Ben's mind the horrible condition of the bridge they had crossed at that town, and he knew there was only one way across the Hudson River at Glens Falls, and that was over ice, but would the ice be thick enough to handle the

148

weight of oxen and sleds loaded with artillery, and of course the Old Sow?

149

CHAPTER TWELVE

They had to wait out the weather and Mother Nature—three days of waiting in Glens Falls for a break to get below zero temperatures and a large enough buildup of ice on the big river. It was finally agreed upon that the Knox train soldiers would go to work on a little known but local method of 'building an ice road bridge' across the river, and not to wait for Mother Nature any longer. The method consisted of marking the straightest route across from shore to shore, and for men to go out onto the ice, admittedly thin ice, and drill holes on both sides of the marked path they meant to take over the ice. In drilling these holes, the river would spew forth her water under such pressure as to send it cascading across the marked path. With each successive layer of water bubbling up and over the path, they would build an ice bridge, supposedly thick enough and strong enough to withstand and bear the weight of the loads they intended to take across the mighty Hudson here at Glens Falls. To do so would put them on the opposite shore and pointed in the right direction.

The work was no easy task, but the men took to it, preferring it to sitting idle. Several days had already been lost, so everyone was anxious to give the trick of the locals and old timers a go. With so many men planting so many holes in the ice, the geysers were everywhere bubbling over the path. Men with a great deal of experience in dealing with

150

ice and icy conditions took soundings and determined the growing thickness of the path Knox's train must not veer from. A foot or two on either side could mean death to men and animals, as well as a loss of artillery.

It would take another day or more to complete the ice bridge. Meanwhile, camp consisted of multiple bonfires and cooking fires for the men. Fires lit up Glens Falls as never before, and many of the townspeople came down to the camp with offerings of biscuits, gravy, venison, and rabbit stew, vegetables and apples. Gill was going about trying to boost the spirit of the camp, jokingly saying, "It's cold enough to freeze the campfire, so why not the river?"

Amid all this comradely warmth, Ben, for the first time, wondered if they had any chance whatsoever in delivering the guns intact, before the British at Boston might overrun Washington's troops there. The thought made for a restless sleep at best.

Knox had a team of men with lanterns working on the ice bridge idea overnight, however, determined to make this 'folklore' a reality, and the science behind it, water under pressure of ice appeared to be working as by sunup, a single oxen pulling a pair of howitzers on a sled with Henry Knox himself walking ahead of the oxen, guiding the animal, while a drover with a whip walked alongside, encouraging the animal to continue across the ice. Knox was doing it—making for the other side of the river over the ice bridge. Knox still had men even now creating new holes on either side for more water to freeze along the bridge path. All of the ice holes froze over if not kept open.

The thinking was if Knox could drive a single sled over successfully, that they could take the oxen over singly pulling the sleds, thus reducing the weight on the ice bridge. He planned to leave the Old Sow for the last crossing. Everyone held his breath until Knox's trial sled made it across to the other side of the wide river. It worked!

Slowly, as the *Cannoneers* dug deep for courage, the artillery train again began moving, bottle-neck fashion across the ice bridge. Each sled's load had been reduced, each pulled by a single oxen rather than two now at a time now, and each made it successfully across the Hudson River. This, everyone knew, meant a great success for Knox's train. They also knew now how to more safely cross other bodies of water that lay ahead of the train. Everyone knew they must cross this same river again twenty miles south at Cohoes Falls and New City, where the river met with the Mohawk River. The waters there would not be so still. So, up 'til now, no one was cheering and would not do so until all the sleds and artillery had been taken across the ice bridge.

Everyone was braced for the Old Sow cracking the ice and falling through when her time came. Ben watched as more icy water bubbled up and men scooped it into buckets to fill in the ruts from the sleds that had already crossed the ice route. Many felt that Knox, who had come walking back across the ice, proud and happy at the results so far, would not chance the Old Sow, that he'd leave word that it was a gift he must leave General Schuyler to deal with. But Henry had no such thoughts troubling him, and he in fact gave a little speech about faith, and then he ordered the Old Sow to be trundled across the ice bridge.

His men remained reluctant and no one volunteered to take the Old Sow across until Ben stepped forward and did so. Gill immediately, like a hovering father, insisted that he would do the honors instead. "Ned and me," he added, volunteering his old friend.

Ned shook his head. "I ain't that dumb, Gill. This is not work for a man who can't swim."

Effram stepped up and said, "Let's do her, Gill."

With Gill guiding the two oxen required to pull the 44-pounder over the rutted ice bridge, and with Effram encouraging the beasts with a whip alongside the sled, the Old Sow began moving across as men on either side furiously added on more freezing water layers across the path. Knox, who asked no one to do what he himself would not do, helped guide the oxen alongside Gill.

Ben watched, with eyes wide, his pride stinging over how Gill and Henry failed to take him seriously when he had volunteered. Ned, beside Ben now, said in his ear, "You best thank Gill and the Colonel that you're not a part of this craziness."

At the halfway point, everyone heard a crack in the buckling ice, and for a moment all movement everywhere stopped. Knox and Gill froze in place, as did the oxen, and as did the men on both sides of the shore. Then Knox and Gill coaxed the animals forward anew, and the Old Sow went on, and with each foot it gained stronger, thicker ice as it neared shore. In short order, the last of the artillery stood on solid ground across the river, and finally, a huge cheer went up among the men.

Ned slapped Ben on the back and said, "You mighta been a hero if Gill and Knox hadn't taken that from ya, boy!" It was the opposite of what Ned had earlier said, but Ben decided to ignore the remark except to reply with, "I ain't in this for no glory, Ned."

"Sure you are; we all are. Else why're we here?"

"Maybe...maybe some." Ben did not know how to answer this. They were indeed creating history. Knox had told them that the British had brought the guns in via the St. Lawrence Seaway in from the ocean on board ships twice the size of the Finn Hawk. They floated them to Lake Champlain and had but a handful of short portages, while the Knox Artillery Train was a three-hundred mile portage, so to speak.

Word passed down the line that the forward section of the artillery train had come in sight of Saratoga. They had come a mere twenty five miles since Fort George, and it was already Christmas Eve.

Albany still lay some thirty five miles south over roads that amounted to mere wagon ruts— where roads could be found at all, that is. These ruts wound up and down and through the rough mountains like bridle paths, and with the snow cover, they could hardly be followed. Often Knox didn't want to follow them, learning from his scouts that they went far afield. He'd opt for a more direct route, a route the men themselves had to cut and clear in slow progression ahead of the exhausted train of men and animals.

The fact they'd only made Saratoga by Christmas gnawed at Knox's insides, and despite the fact he still rode up and down the length of the train, shouting friendly encouragement to everyone, Ben knew he must be terribly disappointed.

Several hours stretched into bleak nightfall with no stars or moon, and the train had settled into a series of camps all around the woods outside Saratoga. Ben Cross and Will Knox were lying side by side near the fire, too weary to worry about eating when Ned Bottomly came to Will, kneeling beside him.

"William, why's your brother want me?" asked Ned.

"What? I dunno."

"The colonel sent word that I was to meet him here at your camp, Ben, Will."

"I've not heard anything, Ned," replied Ben."

"You sure, boys?"

"Don't know, Ned, but if my brother said he'd be here, he'll be here."

"If he doesn't like the work I'm doing, or the way I'm handling my part...or something I said to one of the men...I just want to know. I may just go back to Ticonderoga with Colonel Allen's men when they turn back...join up with the Green

Mountain boys. Sick of all this hurrying up just so we can sit and wait."

"We've covered a lot of ground, Ned," countered Ben.

Ned took Ben aside and said, "You remember the first night we arrived at Fort George? How dog tired we all were, but Colonel Knox, he sat up all night conversing with a British spy in lockup? That fellow they were sending to a firing squad?"

"A fellow named Andre, yes, Major Andre."

"Knox was a friend of this Andre before the war, and why is it Knox is always writing and sending off dispatches—some as far away as New York City? Ben, it's odd for sure."

"Ned, you can't for a moment think Colonel Knox is some sort of spy. That's a crazy notion!"

"Who better to slow down the artillery train than the man in charge of it?"

"It was Knox's idea to come for the Ticonderoga artillery, Ned."

"A perfect cover for a spy."

Ben shook his head. "You're wrong, Ned. That's impossible."

"His relatives, they're all Tories, Ben."

"His in-laws are, yes, but not his wife, and not him or Will."

Suddenly, someone grabbed Ned by his shoulders and shoved him off. It was Gill, angrily saying, "I told you not to repeat that garbage about Colonel Knox, Ned. You and Effram are going to wind up in a jail cell for spreading lies."

Ned was on one knee where he had landed when Gill shoved him. "I ain't saying anything that hasn't been said or thought by every man here, Gill." Ned, fists clenched, as he got nose-to-nose with Gill, prepared to fight back when the darkness all around them was filled with bells. The bells rang out in the distance and were coming ever closer, with each passing second.

"Sleigh bells?" asked Ben. "On Christmas Day?"

The sound of the bells rang out closer and closer, coming out of the darkness around them when everyone cheered on seeing Colonel Knox arriving in a six-passenger sleigh and tossing large white sacks of venison and shouting, "Merry Christmas! Merry Christmas!" He looked like everyone's idea of Santa Claus himself!

Gill ordered Ned and the boys to keep silent about what they had been discussing. "It's no time to spoil Colonel Knox's party, men! Understood?"

They all agreed to keep mum about the disagreement that had erupted just prior to Knox's arrival. The boys rushed to the sled, while Gill had to shove Ned in the same direction.

"Henry!" William said to his brother. "What's all this?"

"Gifts from the people of Saratoga, boys! Christmas gifts for the soldiers—for you all! Goodwill of the people."

"Not the sleigh, for sure," said Ben, admiring the fine workmanship of the ornate sled.

"No, just on lend lease, you might say. Transportation for the gifts here and for you fellows back to Saratoga with me." Knox busied himself with doling out more packages for the hungry soldiers. "We're riding in style, Will, Ben. You too, Gill, Ned."

"Riding where?" asked Ned, sounding grumpy.

"To Saratoga, of course. It's why I sent word ahead for you all to gather here prepared to go. So climb aboard. Who wants to start with the first carol so as we arrive in good Yuletide fashion at the mayor's door?"

"We have an invite from the mayor?" asked Gill.

"None other. News of the train has preceded us, boys, and we are 'royalty' now!" Knox began singing *Deck the Halls* as the others climbed on board the sleigh and found seats. Henry expertly turned the horse-drawn sleigh and they tore off, kicking up snow on either side of them and leaving a wispy plume of snow in their wake.

"Gentlemen, we are going straight for a fine home-cooked meal on Christmas Eve with the John McNeal family—friends of the mayor who will also be in attendance."

"Who is this McNeal fellow?" asked Ned over the noise of the sleigh bells and caroling boys.

"He's the chairman of the Committee on Safety in Saratoga, Ned."

"Really?" gasped Gill.

"And as such, Mr. McNeal and wife insist that we all sleep in real beds tonight."

"Yahhh-hoo!" replied Gill, slapping Ned on the back.

The others joined in Gill's cheer, and when Knox began a chorus of *Auld Lang Syne*, they all joined in.

Christmas Day arrived, ad it came with a fresh blanket of snow. Lots of big, heavy, fluffy wet flakes fell, until it piled high, approximately two feet deep. The evening meal had been scrumptious, with duck as the main course alongside an array of side dishes. Knox and his men were treated like royalty for their work thus far and for their plan to get the cannons into Washington's hands.

By mid-morning, the group had returned to camp to learn that the soldiers had already prepared the oxen teams for travel, but by now the two feet of snow had turned to four, making travel with such a caravan treacherous. Boulders would be invisible below the snow, as would fallen trees. Those wranglers who understood oxen said that 'Oxen don't like snow that fights back'. By early afternoon, the snow was chest high on a short man.

Before long all the Christmas cheer was gone, replaced by surliness among the men; most were understandably upset and angry, feelings that traveled the length and breadth of the train. This ugliness of spirit spread like bad news, and it somehow even seemed to affect the animals. The caravan had traversed a mere eight miles when men began to mutter among themselves. Soon after the men stopped in any further attempt to push their teams forward another step since the oxen had decided for them that *they* weren't taking another step. The entire train ground to a halt, and the standstill was in the middle of nowhere.

Traveling on Christmas Day—as much as they needed to make up lost time—had turned into a kind of curse, it would seem. Colonel Knox rode relentlessly up and down the line, and Ben felt a pang of sorrow to hear him repeatedly shouting for the men to push on without getting the response he wanted from the soldiers.

"You've done well, lads!" he encouraged his men. "This is a sad way to spend Christmas Day, I well know!"

Finally, even Henry saw the writing on the wall as it were, and he capitulated to the oxen as had his men, saying, "All right, fellows, we'll have to be content and happy with the miles we've come today already. All's well…we get up our fires here. Make camp. Tomorrow, lads, we make it to New City."

Ben thought it wise that Henry did not push the issue any further. Given the weather, pushing on, they'd be lucky to make a ninth mile from this day. Ben also realized that Knox had a marvelous gift for insight into the men and leadership qualities that could not be measured, even if he was only twenty-five years old. It was odd, Ben thought, how all of the older soldiers, who had far more experience, respected Henry. No one seemed to think him too young, too inexperienced, or too soft for the role he found himself in. Ben smiled at this thought, and he realized that his friend and leader, Knox, was gifted with firmness, fairness, and resolve when necessary and gentleness when called for—and he had the wisdom to know when each was required.

Another grueling day of backbreaking toil came on December 26th of 1775, a day that would be well-remembered as a true horror by the

Cannoneers themselves. The snow had not gone away, and had in fact frozen over. The ice built up around the sled runners and had to be pounded off by hammers every quarter of a mile, slowing progress down to a crawl. Ben watched all around him as men picked their way foot-by-foot, yard-by-yard, their boots breaking through the ice-encrusted, wet snow with each footfall. William busily sketched such scenes from his perch on one of the sleds, chronicling the events of the day. Today's work was made more difficult as some men had disappeared—*deserted* in the night, unable to take another day of this work, which meant those remaining had to pick up the slack. Many of the men even today had been seen whispering in conspiratorial little groups, no doubt speaking of the possibility of doing the same as their *wiser* brethren—but desertion also branded a man as a coward.

Forage for the animals had become scarce, 'And a hungry ox will always refuse work', as the knowledgeable men said. Knox had sent out foraging parties, but little of worth to feed the livestock had been found, and now the rations for the men, too, were quickly disappearing. Foodstuffs would most certainly be exhausted before they reached Albany. For this reason, New City became Knox's new hope.

The colonel sent a rider ahead of them with a letter signed by McNeal and addressed to the head of the Committee for Safety in New City, but the messenger came straggling back on foot with a horror story of having been waylaid by highwaymen who'd stolen his horse and anything he had of value on him. This meant the letter had gone undelivered.

Somehow, and no one knew for sure just how, they made it to New City in the middle of the night. At least the first sled in the long, disjointed, disorganized train had come to a stop at a place called Mohawk River Landing where the Mohawk met the larger Hudson River. Those men in front of the line now looked out over a huge, snow-covered, ice-packed Mohawk River, but within a stone's throw, the roaring waters of the Hudson flowed unabated, bubbling over rock and slapping at her sides.

Word came down the line to Ben, Will, and the others that their planned for Mohawk River crossing, so long contemplated by everyone, appeared impossible, and that they were again at a standstill.

Ben and Gill made their way to the front of the caravan for a look; this was a trek of three miles, but even though tired, Ben wanted to see firsthand at daybreak what kind of obstacle they now faced. When they arrived, sunlight was on the horizon.

"I can't believe it's not frozen solid, Ben!" Gill said, tearing off his hat and rubbing his hand over his head.

"I know. We've had so many days with freezing temperatures."

"Takes more time in the Mohawk Valley, Ben, but yeah…this is a definite surprise."

"Time," began Ben, "like everything else we need, but have too little of."

"I couldn't agree with you more, Ben," said Henry Knox, who'd come alongside them, his face crestfallen.

With the caravan stuck and no place to go, and with nightfall and boredom having descended upon the camp, Ben now wandered from campfire to campfire, unofficially taking the pulse of the men and planning to report back to Henry on morale among them, he took in the situation with eyes wide open. Each camp had little in the way of rations where men huddled about their fires for warmth, but most seemed bent on bolstering the spirits of one another. *A good sign.* The crackling fires illuminated the condition of the sleds, the animals, and the men. Some sleds were broken and in need of repair, while others had already been hastily patched together. Some sleds had bent runners by now. At the same time, the oxen were somewhat bent and crooked as well, as Ben could see nothing but apathy in their sunken eyes. Here and there an animal was down—and would likely have to be shot and left behind after its meat was harvested. By now Ben had already eaten enough oxen meat to last him a lifetime. Where one ox went by the wayside, another one needed to pull his weight as well as the others. No saboteur could do as much harm to the train as Mother Nature herself had already done, adding great suffering to the hard-won miles.

As Ben was making his rounds this way, suddenly two figures caught his eye; they were both deep in conversation and deep shadow just the other side of the large Old Sow sled. They seemed to be talking heatedly at one moment, then noticing Ben's approach, they fell silent and the taller of the two dashed off into the surrounding forest. He wore a black cape that made him appear to be a mere shadow more than a man in the dim light. The other man began shouting, "Quitter, coward, deserter! Come back!"

Ben recognized Ned Bottomly's voice. Ben rushed to Ned, asking, "Who's run off, Ned?"

"*Ahhh*…just another useless volunteer from Saratoga. Says he's had enough. Didn't get his name. Did my best to get him to stay, but no. Can't say as I blame him."

"Hopefully, we'll have some new volunteers and new sleds in New City," Ben replied.

"Gotta get back to my campfire, Ben. I've got a chill in my bones!"

"Yeah, it's cold all right. Wish that river would cooperate, so we can cross tomorrow."

"It might take days before it's safe to cross with the cannons, Ben."

Then Ned rushed away, seeking that campfire he so wanted.

The following day, Ben again returned to the headwaters of the Hudson where the Mohawk spilled into her. A large number of the soldiers, Gill, and Knox were already there and staring out at the rivers, gauging and studying them in turn. Ben saw now what he'd been told to be true. That while the Mohawk looked frozen over, her waters were still running hard and fast into the Hudson beneath the layer of ice that had formed over her. It was hardly stable ice or thick enough for a man and a horse to walk across, let alone men with oxen and sleds pulling the weight of cannons.

Ben saw that Knox was talking to a stranger, a man Ben had never seen before, a man of New City. Could this be the leader of the Committee for Safety? Had Knox hand-delivered that letter of introduction himself to the New City man? It appeared so. The stranger did a lot of listening, nodding, pointing, and gesturing. The total effect was one that seemed to say that Knox was crazy, Ben thought when suddenly Henry got onto his white horse and started across the Mohawk ice. Everyone fell silent at the sight.

Henry did not simply walk the animal across the ice; he did not even cantor or trot across to get to the safety of the other side. He had chosen a section approximately two hundred yards from where the Hudson met the Mohawk and there he had his horse rise up on her haunches and slam her hooves into the ice repeatedly. He then rode about in a wide circle, the mare slamming the ice as they went. It was a show of faith that they could take the cannon across at the place where Knox rode.

It would require cutting a path to get to this section of frozen river. Some men among the soldiers instantly realized this and set to work felling trees and moving stones in the path, while others still balked at the idea of going across the Mohawk at all until it was more solidly frozen over. Some said that the colonel's little show was no matter, and that while he was a big man, he was not heavy as the Old Sow.

165

Knox returned to his men and shouted from his horse, "Men, if the temperature drops overnight, and I am sure it will, we've got our passage to the other side."

Ned shouted next to the men, "I think that was the bravest thing I ever saw a man do!" He indicated Knox on horseback.

Knox laughed and raised a hand and shook his head self-deprecatingly. "Not bravery, Ned, just determination. Besides, before I did it…before you men were awake, we took soundings. The ice is a good three inches thick now. By morning, we should be able to create an ice bridge as we did before, remember?"

This all to the dull rhythm of the waters of the Mohawk meeting those of the Hudson mere feet from where they all stood.

The New City man who had thought Knox mad to think he could take cannons across the Mohawk tomorrow ambled off, shaking his head, while Ben Cross felt a distinct new kind of cold scratching at his skin, an arctic cold. For once, perhaps the weather was in fact willing to cooperate with the men of the train.

The following day, the entire train started across the ice in the early morning hours. Other than an occasional oxen stopping to sit square on the ice in the middle of the route across the river, the caravan completed the Mohawk crossing without delay or incident. Once across, however, the Knox Train remained in New City for two days, as it required that much time to replenish supplies, make sled repairs, and locate additional oxen, and men willing to fill the ranks of the teamsters.

For Ben and Will, the long delay felt like a double-edged sword; on the one hand, it meant a delay in getting to their final destination, but on the other, it meant rest and recuperation. Some of the men needed medical attention as well, as an epidemic of pneumonia had run the length of the train.

When the Knox Train finally got underway again, they soon found themselves passing through a dense forested wilderness wherein the oxen's shoulders touched trees on either side. Far ahead of Ben and the others, he could hear the cry of TIMBER, which could be heard for miles as advance teams felled trees. At the same time, the snow here was like a fine, woolen blanket, untouched. It was also the deepest, heaviest snow they had faced to date.

Coming alongside Ben where he sat on a sled, driving a team of oxen, Knox tipped his hat to Ben. "We've come a long journey together already, Ben. I appreciate your grit and determination." By late afternoon, Knox's horse had become too exhausted to take one more step in the deep snow. The white mare tried valiantly to pull ahead once more, but she simply could not. It was at this point that Knox dismounted, un-cinched the animal, tossed the saddle and blanket onto Ben's sled. He said of his horse, "She's done for, Ben."

"Are you sure, sir?"

"Afraid so, yes."

167

Ben looked back at the regal, white mare with sadness as they continued on without her. He recalled how far she'd carried Knox—from Cambridge to Ticonderoga and all this way back. Against the whiteness of the land, as the sled moved off, the mare faded and disappeared.

"Perhaps she may have a chance to find her way to one of the farms we passed outside New City," Henry said in a consoling tone.

"I know she will," Ben replied.

Suddenly, Ben had to pull up on his reins, stopping the brutish oxen team, and he and Knox stared at the sled ahead of them which had halted. The teamster cracked his bullwhip over the ears of his team, but his oxen refused to take another step. Like the mare, they'd had enough. They were not going to move a muscle. Instead, they nestled down into the snow where they stood.

Knox climbed down and rushed to the front. He and several other men began pulling from the front, while another continued cracking the whip, and yet another was throwing wood chips into the backsides of the beasts. Nothing moved the animals. No amount of coaxing was working when Ben's team decided to do the same where they stood.

Not even the barking of the camp dogs could budge the exhausted oxen, and now a chain reaction occurred. Team after team dropped and nestled into the ground where they were. It was an oxen work strike. Then for no apparent reason, some of the soldiers began throwing snowballs at one another, the missiles flying in all directions, laughter erupting all around. A frolicking snowball fight was in full swing. The snowball fight lasted some fifteen or twenty minutes, and Knox and Ben were in the thick of it as it had exploded all around them. The laughter of the men echoed through the woods.

CHAPTER THIRTEEN

Somehow in using tender words with their oxen, the more experienced teamsters got the oxen up and moving again the same day. The train marched another two miles through places where a rabbit couldn't go, places so deep with snow as to obliterate any notion of a road. Passing a lonely little farmhouse, Knox called out to the man inside who—*weapon in hand*—stared out in amazement on seeing the mile-long cannon train pass by his door. Knox asked, "Are we on the right road to Squire Jonathan Fisher's house, sir?"

The old farmer laughed. "There ain't no road around here. Not even a cow path."

"Do you know the whereabouts and general direction to Squire Fisher's place?"

The man shook his head doubtfully but pointed and said, "Several miles in the general direction you are pointed, but Fisher's got no use for cannons."

"The squire has promised food and lodging for my men, sir. You have heard of the Army of the Continental Congress, surely."

"No…no, can't say as I have."

"How far ahead to Fisher's did you say?"

"A few miles on. The old fellow has a lot of room, but I doubt he can feed the lot of you." The old farmer ambled back inside his place and watched them from his window until they were out of sight, swallowed again by the forest. As the train

170

moved on, word of how close their next stopover was went down the line.

Ben had never known how long a few more miles could be. He was freezing, and every bone felt like it was set hard, as if his marrow had turned to ice. His teeth were chattering, but he lifted his eyes and tipped back his tri-cornered hat to better see the outline of a large, well-built, warm looking log home rise from the gloom ahead. The house was set off from a large barn and a tack house. He prayed it was the Fisher home when ahead of him, he could hear shouts that they'd found Squire Fisher.

Ben was soon close enough to see a stubby, round man in thick coat and hat who'd rushed out to greet them, waving madly and directing traffic, telling Knox where to rest his animals and men. Ben decided the barn would be home for the night, and he appreciated it as if it were a palace. It was a barrier against the wind, and with all the men and animals sharing space, it would be a hot house of sorts. Then Ben was surprised when Fisher insisted every one of them come up to the house for hot tea, calling them all patriots.

Before dawn the Knox Artillery Train was underway, continuing its journey to the next destination: Albany, New York. Hope ran high that they'd make the city before nightfall, as this meant plenty of shelter, warm food, a place for every man to comfortably sleep under a roof, plus the support and help of General Schuyler's entire command. Many of the men who'd volunteered and who had homes in and around Fort Ticonderoga, Lake

George, Glens Falls, having come the entire way, now planned to return to their families once Knox's cannons were safely in Albany. As a result, there was an air of excitement and cheerfulness this morning, until word came from the rear of the train, from Ned Bottomly's section.

A boy named Davey Becker had arrived with the news. Having been sent by his teamster father, Davey reported the first desertion from the soldiers' ranks. All previous desertions had come from the citizens and the volunteer ranks. The real blow was that this deserter's name was Ned Bottomly.

Private Bottomly, who'd been made a corporal by Knox, was gone in the night—disappeared without neither a word nor a trace. He must be presumed a deserter from the army. It was a blow that nearly felled Gill McCleary, who took the news harder than Ben, Knox or anyone else. The news sent Gill into a grim and somber mood.

"I should've seen this coming," he muttered to Knox. "I should've known it."

"We've already lost enough time over it, Gill," replied Knox, a hand on Gill's shoulder. He then told Davey Becker that Effram would be in charge of the soldiers and that his father was in charge of the teamsters in that section of the train. "Our first order of business today is to make Albany by nightfall, and there's a storm brewing from the smell in the air."

Knox then rode to the front of the train, having confiscated Ben's horse for his purposes. Ben said to Gill, "Don't blame yourself, Gill. It's not your doing."

172

"I never figured Ned'd do such a fool thing." Gill, shaking his head walked off, shoulders down around his chest.

Colonel Knox refused to let the set-back slow him down. Filled with confidence, his plan was to go in advance of the train to Albany, as he was anxious to report their great progress to General Schuyler. He'd inform the general of their harrowing moments, of course, but also of their present position and estimated time of arrival in Albany.

Before mid-morning, Ben and the others on the train wished that Knox had remained with them. The storm he'd predicted was more than just a storm. The word storm was not nearly strong enough for this Nor'easter as the old-timers called it. It'd begun with a light snowfall, teasing really, but soon grew to a thick, icy attack of pellet-like stony ice. The sleet was blinding and it whipped ferociously behind sixty-mile an hour winds, causing the world to become one white and blinding place in which no ox and no man could see.

The animals balked and stuttered, then stopped altogether, and the sleds came apart when men, anxious to make Albany, pushed ahead against better judgment. Most of the cannons became bogged down or half-tipped over along the side of the now invisible roads outside Albany. Some five miles from the city, the entire train became stranded. Nothing could move. Every sled and animal pulling it were now in ditches, blindly led to this fate.

Stopped cold, the guns looked sad and useless—like so much discarded pig iron strewn about the woods. Gill rode the length of the train on horseback now, shouting something as he approached Ben's position. Gill gave everyone a choice. Any man who wished to stay with the cannons through the night could do so; he wanted volunteers. Any man who wished to walk into Albany and stay the night there, he gave the go ahead. It was still daylight, nearing six o'clock, but the cannons would have to be abandoned until morning.

Almost every man opted for Albany with a dry bed and a roof overhead. When the men began walking off, leaving the mile-long artillery train behind, Ben thought the guns truly looked abandoned. Ben, Gill, William, the Beckers, father and son, and a handful of others decided to build a fire and stay with the guns and the animals.

Even before daybreak the following day, strange reports began to trickle into camp. The ridiculous story said that Colonel Henry Knox was locked up in a cell at Schuyler's orders, locked away in the cell block at the fort in Albany. It made no sense whatsoever, as he had been arrested on charges of treason!

A second report said that the authorities believed Knox was a Tory and a British spy, and that he had intentionally sabotaged his own artillery train from the beginning, including the sinking of one cannon at Sabbath Day Point.

Ben was incensed at the notion. "That's crazy! Henry wasn't even with us at Sabbath Day when that happened! That's like blaming the weather on him."

"We know better, Ben," Gill assured him. "There's got to be a mistake in all this. There just has to be."

Effram had brought them the news. "Just tellin' you what the scuttlebutt is, Gill. Word is, who better to slow the train than a spy put in charge of it all?"

A soldier with Effram shook his head and added, "They're talking court martial in the town."

"Court martial?" William rushed at the soldier, fists ready to rain blows on him when Gill grabbed him up.

"Don't shoot the messenger," said Effram.

"And if he's found guilty," continued the other soldier, "they could stand him up for a firing squad, unless they trade him in a prisoner exchange."

"Hold on a minute," said Gill to a struggling William. "What'd you say before, Effram?"

"I didn't say it! I know it's a lie."

"But what you said—who better than the man in charge to slow the train down."

"You're not agreeing with them, are you, Gill?" asked Ben.

"Of course not, but it bears some thinkin' time. "Don't you boys recall last time you heard words like that?"

Ben wracked his brain for what Gill referred to. "Ned! That's almost word for word what Ned once suspected of Henry—*ahhh*, Colonel Knox."

175

"And now it's being repeated all over Albany," replied Gill. "A rumor is an ugly thing that takes on a life of its own. Ned may have been talking for no good reason but now it's come home to roost."

"You don't suppose Ned's somewhere in Albany, do you?" asked Will. "If we could drag him to the general and explain this nonsense then maybe…just maybe…"

Gill considered this for only a moment, pulling at his beard. "I suspect Ned is nowhere near Albany. He likely took off straight up north, back-tracking along our path. I figure he'd be one to join up with the Green Mountain Boys back at Fort Ti."

"Are you going to fetch him back here, Gill? We might need him to testify on the colonel's behalf." Ben's question was half plea, half demand for Gill to do just that.

"Ned always liked the idea of going chasing into Canada with Colonel Allen. I'll chase him down, catch him, and drag him back here, and I won't come back without him."

"I'll go with you," suggested Ben.

Gill shook his head. "No, this is between me and Ned. You boys get to Albany, see the colonel, and tell him of our suspicions. I'll be back as soon as I can."

"Gill…the night Ned disappeared, I saw him talking with someone, arguing really, and the other man ran off soon as I came near."

"Who was it?"

"I didn't get a good look at him, but he wore a big, black cape…like the sort a soldier might own, an officer."

"Hmmm…Ned in argument with this man, an officer?"

"Yes, and it was quite heated."

Gill nodded and was quickly on his way, taking the horse with him. With Ned afoot, Gill had a good chance of catching up with the other man. Almost the moment Gill disappeared in the distance, Ben and Will heard horses coming from the direction of Albany, straight for them. It was a regiment of soldiers galloping down on them. They dismounted and began the work of reclaiming the cannons from their stranded positions along the ditches and gullies. The soldiers were under the command of Major John Pritchett, wearing his finest uniform and black cape. His orders resounded through the silent forest, and his men claimed control of the oxen and the train. Mr. Becker was shoved aside, while Effram caught the butt of an army rifle for standing in the way. Pritchett would have his way, and suddenly everything seemed clear to Ben.

Ben shared his suspicion that it had been Pritchett all along, and that somewhere along the line, he'd gotten Ned involved in his scheme to take over the train. Henry had been right about the man all along. He wanted to be the one to personally gift the artillery over to General Washington; he wanted the glory of that moment and any possible rewards such as a bump in rank. It had apparently become the major's primary goal in life.

"I suspect Pritchett got to Ned during the down time when we first came through Albany," suggested Will.

"And I suspect it was Ned who cut the rope at Sabbath to send that 24-pounder into the drink."

"We were all looking forward to a great welcoming party in Albany, but never a necktie party," said Will, dispirited.

"Some welcome all right."

Major Pritchett ignored the boys, riding the length of the train, shouting orders as his men formed into teams and harnessed the reluctant oxen unused to their hands, odors, or voices. Pritchett shouted, "Get this pile of iron moving! I want this artillery in Albany as it should have been before these men abandoned it."

Pritchett's men moved like soldiers who took orders well. Meanwhile, Knox's remaining, curious men were told to disperse to their homes or regiments by order of General Schuyler. Some of the Knox men needed no second telling, having planned on leaving the train by this time anyway. But most walked in circles, unsure of what to do, and the teamsters were not about to leave their animals in the hands of these men who did not understand the beasts, nor their needs.

With Knox and Gill both gone now, some of the train men and New Hampshire soldiers came to Ben to ask what they should do.

"Do what you wish, but my brother is innocent of these ugly charges!" shouted William at the men.

Ben tried to calm Will, and to calm the men as well. "Will and me, we're going to Albany to stand by Colonel Knox. If there's to be a trial, I want to give testimony. How about you men?"

178

Everyone present cheered this idea. In a solid group, Ben, Will, Effram, and the others all marched for Albany.

It was nightfall before Gill McCleary wandered into Ned Bottomly's camp, where dirt and ashes had been quickly scattered over the smoldering embers. Ned had tried to hide his trail, but a man on foot usually leaves clues, and Gill was a master tracker. The snow also made the job of tracking a man that much easier.

Judging by the still burning embers of Ned's fire, Gill felt certain that Ned was within earshot and likely had by now drawn a bead on whoever was on his trail. Gill simply went to the fire, threw some twigs onto the dying thing and revived it, kneeling the entire time, remaining silent, allowing Ned to see that it was his friend who'd come for him. A few healthy, hungry flames licked up high now as the fire grew as Gill built it up to a respectable level. Gill was a hunter, and he knew when and how to let his prey come to him. Eventually, he heard Ned off to his left, stepping softly into the fire glow. His features were cut in half by the darkness, but there was no mistaking that it was Ned, looking like a man in despair.

Before Gill had gotten too far on his trek after Ned, Effram had caught up to him to inform him of how Major Pritchett had taken complete charge of the artillery train. Gill was now sitting cross-legged at the fire, and he softly said to his longtime friend, "Did ya hear that Colonel Knox was arrested for being a British spy, Ned? And that Major Pritchett

179

has taken over running the train the rest of the way to Boston?"

Ned inched around Gill with great care, finally sitting across from him Indian fashion at the campfire. "I-I tried to tell you that Knox couldn't be trusted, Gill."

"Guess you were right, Ned. But desertion? Why didn't you talk to me first?"

"You'd have stopped me."

"I mighta, yes, the way I was feeling about the colonel and our grand business...the business of getting the guns to Washington. We sure got ourselves into a passel of work and worry, eh, Ned?"

"We sure did. Did you come alone, or did Effram come, too? Is he out there with a gun trained on me?"

"There's nobody here but you and me, my friend, so you can loosen your grip on that squirrel gun."

Ned relaxed his grip and put the gun aside. "Then Major Pritchett was right about Knox all along, huh?"

"I don't know. What did the major tell you, Ned, the night Ben saw you arguing with him? The night you ran off?"

"He told me to keep an eye on Knox. He knew about Knox's having sat up all night conversing with that traitor Major Andrea at the fort."

"What else?"

"The major, he said the guns would be safer if they were in General Schuyler's hands and under his control."

180

"I see. But explain to me why he asked you to sabotage the train at Sabbath Point, Ned? How would that help anybody?"

"I ain't saying I did that, Gill."

"Someone cut the rope, Ned, and young Ben and I figure it was you."

"I wasn't even at Sabbath Day Point, Gill."

"Neither was Knox!"

They fell into a glum silence and watched the flames. After a moment, Gill surmised aloud, "The major said he needed time to get up enough dirt on Knox before we got the train to Albany, I suppose, eh?"

"It all figures that way, Gill. Pritchett says that Henry Knox is at heart a…a Tory, and that for his entire life he's been on the side of British home rule, and his wife was raised a Tory, and his in-laws, so why would he change? It's to do with the guns, Gill. It makes more sense that he comes up here, a bookseller, to this kind of life and to this territory, not to help out at Boston but to help the British hold onto Boston *instead*!"

Gill imagined Pritchett sneaking about, pouring poisonous lies into Ned's ear. "You were to make the trek from Ticonderoga to Albany a complete disaster, so they'd have to take the guns out of Knox's control. Well…it sure worked out—all of Pritchett's lies."

"They don't sound like lies the way Pritchett tells it, Gill. He has a heap of facts he's collected on Knox's movements. How he was able to go in and out of Boston when no one else could, that kind of thing."

181

"Do you still believe that man's stories about the colonel?" Gill's tone took on a protective strength. "You know I've always done right by you, Ned, and I've always helped you out, but honestly, I think you were snookered by the major."

"I thought you was being Knox's fool all that time," he replied.

"I should've paid more heed to what was going on in your head, partner, and I know you tried to tell me. I just didn't realize how…well, how far gone you were on this game of Pritchett's."

"You were a might busy, after all," Ned allowed.

The two old friends stared into one another's eyes. "A lot's changed since we left home in New Hampshire, Ned."

"That's the truth."

"But I haven't, not in here." Gill beat his chest. "And neither has it in you."

"That's the truth," Ned repeated.

"I think when you choose to put your trust in a man, it ought to be rewarded, but Ned, I also think you put your trust in the wrong man this time around."

Ned sat silent for a time at this. "I feel I can't trust nobody no more."

"You can trust me." Gill shrugged and threw another branch onto the fire, sending up fiery sparks. "Tell me about every meeting you had with the major and what was said."

"It's too late to fix things, Gill. Knox, you say is locked up and waiting on a trial, and Pritchett has control of the train."

"It's not too late. Not if you come back with me."

"I'd be made a fool in a courtroom, and you know it."

"Not so! Pritchett is as smooth as a snake with a forked tongue, Ned. He fooled a general, General Schuyler, same as you. If you come back and tell the court about how the major talked you into it, you'd be doing the right thing, the patriotic thing. Knox should not be suffering like this."

"I feel bad about it; I didn't know how far Pritchett would take it."

"He's trying to see that Henry Knox is hanged or shot as a spy, Ned. Tell me, did he pay you in coin?"

"He did."

"That's even more damning if you come back with me and tell it to the general if not the court."

"Who's going to believe me over a major?"

"Me for one, all the men on the train for another, Knox, his little brother, the teamsters, maybe General Schuyler as well."

"You think so?"

"I know so, and I think we should start heading back now, tonight."

Ben Cross had almost given up on finding Gill McCleary and Ned Bottomly. Ben had tracked Gill from Albany, following as best he could on a broken down old mare—as Gill had taken the only remaining good horse, as Ben's mare—as with all the livestock of the train—was confiscated, locked up, so to speak, along with Colonel Knox.

183

Ben had come through areas where it was unsafe to ride, so often he'd had to lead the horse by hand. He found tell-tale signs of Gill's having passed this way and then that-a-way, when he heard a gunshot and feared the worst, that the two lifelong friends had quarreled and that either Gill or Ned had been shot. He galloped toward the gunshot sound, shouting Gill's name when he came on a clearing where both men were indeed arguing, but arguing over whose shot had brought down a deer. Claiming rights meant skinning rights as well, so they were actually arguing over who had brought down the deer.

Gill saw Ben first and waved and shouted back to him. Ned nervously and shyly looked as if he might bolt for fear of what Ben thought of him, but he stood his ground, and he won the argument, saying, "You do the dressing, and I'll do the cooking." Both men were starving, as was Ben, so they built a fire and shared the venison as there was more than enough for all three. In fact, they had leftovers for the wolves that'd been tracking them.

Gill and Ned had made it three-quarters of the way back to Albany when Ben had stumbled upon them here. Around the campfire they'd built, the three friends said little but ate heartily when the meat had been fully cooked through. Ben finally said to Gill, "It occurred to me that you might need help."

"It did, did it?" asked Gill around a mouthful of venison.

"Yes, sir. It surely did occur to me! Feared the worst, I did."

184

"Don't worry. Ned here's had a favorable change of heart."

CHAPTER FOURTEEN

Military court proceedings, called a court martial, like a firing squad, always began at dawn, and Colonel Henry Knox's court martial was no exception. By the time Ben and Gill made it back to the fort at Albany, New York, the trial was well underway, and it was going badly for Henry. Ben watched Gill part a crowd of Knox men standing around the headquarters where, on the inside, the proceedings were being held. Two guards stopped Gill in his tracks at the door. "You have to let us inside, soldier," Gill said. "We have evidence important to the trial."

All the Knox men, hearing this, and seeing that Ned had returned, crowded in on the two guards, and when the guards refused to allow Gill, Ben, and Ned to enter, the Knox men took control of the guards, taking their weapons and pretty much sitting on the men.

When Ben, Gill, and a reluctant Ned finally got into the actual court martial proceedings, Ben heard the prosecutor snidely saying, "But you were a bookseller in Boston before the outbreak of war, sir."

This comment had the officers at the judges table whispering to one another.

Knox, speaking from the witness stand, replied, "An honest profession, sir."

186

"And one riddled with debt, as well as the possibility of having ties to the British, no doubt," countered the prosecution.

Ben, Gill, and Ned had wisely entered the courtroom come as quietly as possible, finding seats in the gallery.

"If you are implying that I would let my outstanding bills direct my politics and allegiances, sir, then you are *completely and utterly* mistaken."

This drew laughter from the gallery, and the gavel came down hard for order even though the judge with gavel in hand was nodding and smiling as if he wanted to chuckle as well.

The prosecutor ignored it entirely, saying, "It's true then that you were in grave debt to British merchants for books, paper, and other supplies?"

"Every merchant in Boston was in debt to merchants in Britain," Knox fired back.

"We here today refer only to you, sir!" replied the prosecuting officer, a raw-boned, lanky fellow under Major Pritchett's command.

Ben noticed Pritchett, or rather the back of his head, where he sat directly behind the prosecutor's table and chair.

Knox was now saying, "My British partners and creditors were reasonable men, patient, and they always got their due. Some were kind and patient to a fault."

"*Ahhh*, indeed!" replied the prosecutor, nodding as if he had uncovered some buried truth. "Then you did have strong ties with the British."

"Civilians, yes, military, no."

187

Ben noticed a piece of paper with writing on it was being passed now from judge to judge, all five of the uniformed men making faces over what appeared to be a list of the charges against Henry. Ben next saw General Schuyler was in a special seat, observing the proceedings but remaining silent.

"My largest debts came about in my binding and publishing business, largely due to the cost of printing pamphlets calling for fairness from Britain. Then later pamphlets calling for *revolution* with Britain!" Knox said in his defense. "I carried patent medicines, breads, baskets, flutes, telescopes, and wall paper as well as books, gentlemen. Merely a businessman."

"Some here have testified that all the printing and publishing you did before the war broke out was conservative in tone, influenced by Toryism."

Knox gritted his teeth and shook his head. "I printed whatever an author brought to my door. I did not write it, nor did I feel it my position to change a word of it or ban it from my shop. I was hoping to one day publish a newspaper."

Knox turned from the prosecutor and spoke directly to the judges, adding, "Sirs, I may well have been in some debt, just as all Boston was yoked to Britain's taxes and economic woes, but I would not sell my country for the difference ever!"

The piece of paper that the judges had been passing around went to General Schuyler now, and on reading it, he stood and addressed Henry directly. "Colonel Knox, more to the point, we have documented evidence that as early as 1766 at a time when you were a boy of sixteen, you trained with British regulars. Is *this* true?"

"Trained? At sixteen? With regulars?" Knox was stunned that such a question could be leveled at him with the barbs it entailed.

"Come, don't be evasive with this court, Colonel." Schuyler wanted a better answer for certain.

The chief judge, gavel at hand, added, "We know you have had frequent contact with British soldiers and not just British merchants and merchant ships, sir."

"1766, really?" asked Knox with a shake of the head. "It was an entirely different world, ten years ago." Knox laughed at some memory of that time.

"You find this court amusing, Colonel?" asked Schuyler, and Ben could see Pritchett's smile even though he could only see the back of the man's head.

"Sir, General, you are referring to a band of boys who made guns from tree limbs and marched about the parade ground, playacting and some of the soldiers took pity on us, took us under wing, and drilled us proper till we fell out!" Knox smiled at the memory of the boyhood adventure. "And they gave us lessons on how artillery worked. For the soldiers, it broke the monotony of their time away from home, for we boys, it was heavenly fun."

"Boyhood play-acting, eh?" Mr. Prosecutor asked in a snakelike voice.

"That band of soldiers were headed for Quebec," said Knox. "Going forth to protect us all from aggression and death at the hands of the

189

French and Indians. They were going forth to fight and possibly die for Boston, for Massachusetts and for all the colonies. They were, in our eyes, *heroes*."

"I do recall it was a terrible winter in '66," Schuyler thoughtfully said, still standing. "Those soldiers coming through at Boston were delayed for over a month…and many died in battle."

"A fine bunch of fellows they were, General," said Knox.

"You do not help your case by praising British soldiers, Colonel," said the prosecutor.

"Those soldiers at that time, sir, were *our* soldiers, and we were *all*, at that time, sir, British citizens." Knox straightened up where he sat. "Their soldiers at the time mingled with our soldiers and officers. There was no animosity among them."

"Our soldiers?" asked the prosecutor.

"The men of the Boston Train, an artillery unit made up of men from the Commonwealth of Boston. We all had the love of artillery in common."

"How was this artillery train in Boston organized?" asked Schuyler.

"The British supplied the artillery and the tools, sir, and often a British officer would oversee the training, but it was all for the home protection of our town, approved by the colonial legislature, and in cooperation with the British garrison in Boston."

"Yes, I see…ten years ago," replied Schuyler.

"As you know, militia companies like the Minute Men were formed up and down the seaboard in every colony when the French, our common enemy roused the natives against us. This was years before hostilities erupted between the Crown and the colonies."

"What of this drillmaster you had as a boy," asked one of the judges. "This Major Bradley."

"Bradley of the British Regulars," said Knox, smiling. "A fine man, sirs. The epitome of the British soldier, and he taught us all valuable lessons that have more than once saved my life."

The prosecutor jumped on this statement. "What sort of lessons?"

"Why…lessons on the proper handling and care of artillery. If you fail to swab out, the barrel overheats, and you could spend the rest of your life a broken man in bandages—if not killed outright by the big gun."

"And where is your Major Bradley now?"

"I have no idea. I suppose he is in New York. He's not in Boston."

"*Ahhh*, yes, New York—where you recently visited."

"I went there on orders to inspect the artillery, orders from General Washington. I explained this in detail to General Schuyler."

"To my satisfaction at the time," Schuyler replied, sitting back down.

"I have not seen or spoken to the major since the Battle of Bunker Hill."

"Aha, then you spoke to him during the battle at Bunker Hill?"

"No, since before Bunker Hill, since before hostilities broke out." Knox sounded exasperated, and Ben could well understand why.

Gill nudged Ben and pointed to the other side of the gallery at young William Knox who looked ready to leap up and shout at the judges and the prosecutor, who was now saying, "It is a matter of record that many of you Boston men in this Train you speak of—that they were offered commissions in the British army and navy, and that many of the men you trained with over the past ten years accepted those commissions. How are we to believe that one of your Artillery Train members has not been turned out as a spy, Colonel Knox? A spy who knows how to destroy a good cannon as much as preserve one?"

"I protest the nature of such a question. I protest to this court, to your honors, that such innuendo and outright allegations brought against me are both absurd and false! And it is extremely difficult to sit here and listen to such rubbish!"

The gallery, half stacked with Pritchett's men and half with Knox's men, erupted in jeers and cheers to which the gavel judge responded, threatening to clear the room at one more outburst. At the same time, Ben's mind raced with the questions taunting him: could Knox be convicted? If so, what will happen to his plans for the cannons? Could Henry be executed on such trumped up charges?

Again General Schuyler stood, calming the room with his presence. He asked Henry point blank, "Colonel Knox, were you offered a commission by the British army to join their ranks?"

"At the outbreak of hostilities, yes. I was offered the enticing rank of Colonel, in fact, and I've made no secret of it. It's why General Washington put the same rank up for me before the Continental Congress—my preference and allegiance is with Boston, Massachusetts and the colonies."

Again the judges whispered among themselves, when young Will Knox lost control of himself and shouted for Henry to "Tell them how you got three 3-pounders out of Boston for the Rebels, Henry! Tell them how hard you worked on the fortifications at Dorchester Heights!"

William was grabbed by the bailiff as the gavel judge ordered him taken out. Will did not go quietly. When the courtroom calmed anew, Mr. Prosecutor said, "Now, Colonel, we get to the matter of your wife, Lucy Whitaker who—"

"I will not stand for anyone disparaging the honor of my wife, sir!" Knox had stood, his face beat red.

"Regain your seat, Colonel!" ordered the gavel judge.

As Knox sat back down, the prosecutor continued. "Lucy Whitaker comes from a well-known Tory family, the daughter of the Royal Secretary of Massachusetts. Is this not so?"

"She has a mind of her own; she is no more Tory than you are, sir."

"Has her father not remained in Boston, a staunch loyalist to the Crown?"

"Yes, but that is her father's choice, not mine!"

193

"And does he not sit in on high-level military strategy meetings in the British camp?"

"I have no such knowledge of that, sir. I also have no idea of where he sits, as I am not married to him."

This brought on laughter, and the gavel judge lifted his gavel but did not drop it. "Continue," he said to the prosecutor.

"You're a smart young man, Colonel Knox. At only age twenty-six is it? To be a colonel in not one but *two* armies?"

"I resent that characterization, sir!"

"So no matter which side wins or loses, Henry Knox wins....either way!"

"You are dangerously close to having to meet me on the field of honor, sir, in a duel," declared Knox, his fists like large balls.

"Will the court please instruct the witness that such threats are—"

"I am no traitor! Nor am I anyone's spy! Nor am I a counter-spy. I hold the confidence of the highest ranking officer in the Continental Army, and when he hears of this...this circus that your Major Pritchett there is the *ringmaster* for, someone will pay dearly, but it won't be me."

"Isn't it true, sir, that your wife is the go-between for you and your father-in-law to pass information on to the British?"

"I will not dignify such lies with an answer." Knox's hands went white where he gripped the chair he sat in.

"Then answer this! At Fort Ticonderoga several British officers were under lock and key, awaiting

194

transportation and to be interrogated by experts, but you chose to visit with them. In fact, you spent an entire evening in the cells with them. Why? What are we to make of such behavior?"

"I went to see Major Andre. Before the war, we were…we were friends."

"*Aha!*"

"Andre has chosen his course. It was in his mind the only course open to him, to side with the British…to become a spy for their cause. However, I have chosen my course—an opposite one to his."

"We questioned Major Andre when he was being transported, during his stopover. He says you two remain fast friends."

"This war has split asunder many families and many friends, sad to say."

"Well your friend did not betray you, Colonel."

"Whatever do you mean?"

"We offered him a chance at prisoner exchange rather than the rope if he would be tell us of your true allegiance."

"He told you the truth then."

"Perhaps…perhaps not."

"A lesser man would have told you a lie to save himself and sacrifice me to the dogs of war."

"Let's turn then to the little matter of a cannon falling into Lake George due to a saboteur, an incident you elected to tell no one about—no reports to General Schuyler or to General Washington on the matter, and no one apprehended for the crime."

"I saw no need of reporting the matter until we had someone apprehended. Be reasonable, sir."

Ben, like Will before him, could contain himself no longer. He leapt up and rushed to the front of the court, shouting, "We watched and waited for the saboteur to strike again, and we caught him after he ran off, and he's here in this room right here, right now!"

The gavel judge was banging away as the gallery went wild with this revelation. "Silence, silence!" the judge said, and when all calmed, he ordered the bailiff, who already had Ben by the scruff of the neck, to remove Ben from the courtroom.

Gill stood and pulled Ned to his feet beside him, saying, "The lad speaks the truth, your honors, and Ned here wants to tell this court he sabotaged the train, but he also wants to tell you at whose orders he did it—Major Pritchett's orders!"

This had everyone in the room bubbling over with curiosity, whispers and gasps. The five judges looked about at one another, and the gavel judge, after conferring with the others ruled that Ben could stay, and that the court would hear Private Ned Bottomly's confession.

But first Major Pritchett rushed forward, protesting the lies and slander of his good name. "This is a preposterous fiction, your honors. These two men have been handpicked from Knox's artillery train. They're in with Knox's schemes! They'll say and do anything to save him from a firing squad."

General Schuyler shouted at Pritchett, "Major, you have quite a low opinion of these men!"

"Yes, sir! You will find Knox's men to all be scoundrels and backwoodsmen, who wouldn't for a moment hesitate to lie for him."

"I was a backwoodsman myself for a while, Major," said Schuyler. "I generally find backwoodsmen to be honest by nature. In any event, let's hear what they have to say. Swear them in, bailiff."

First Gill got his opportunity to give testimony, and he was direct and to the point. He was followed by a shaky Ned, who said that he was angry with himself for having been duped into working on Major Pritchett's behalf, because the major told him all the stories about how Knox had to be an enemy spy. "Forgive me, Colonel Knox, but the major there had my head spinning with all the horrible things you had planned for the artillery. I was supposed to slow the progress of the train long enough for the major to bring charges once we arrived here in Albany." Before his testimony was over, Ned had become tearful, pleading for Knox's forgiveness, which Henry publicly gave. "It's all the truth, sirs, so help me God. I'd become convinced on…on the word of Major Pritchett and all the *evidence* he claimed was real."

"What changed your mind then, Private?" asked the gavel judge.

"After working alongside Colonel Knox, I've come to know the man, and I realized too late that the major there was using me for a fool."

"So you deserted before just Albany, knowing things would go badly for Colonel Knox?" asked the judge.

"God help me, I did. I couldn't see no other way out but to go back and serve under Colonel Allen, my old regiment. So I lit out."

Pritchett stood alone before the court as even the main prosecutor worked to distance himself from him. The judges at the bench, and General Schuyler stared holes through Pritchett, and finally, the general ordered the guards to take the major into custody. "We'll deal with you later, John," Schuyler said with a shake of his grey head.

The court issued an apology to Colonel Knox, then the gavel came down, and the lead judge said, "Case closed! You, sir, are free to go."

Cheers erupted from all the Knox supporters in the room, many of them doing a dance while Henry embraced William, who'd remained at the door, listening in. Ben and Gill joined the reunion, Gill doing a little dance as well, until his eyes fell on his old friend, Ned, who shouted to Knox, "I'm sorry, Colonel, for being such a fool."

"Ned, Pritchett had five judges and a general believing the same of me; not entirely your fault, my friend. I will use all my influence and powers of persuasion to have you back under my command when the artillery train gets underway again, I promise."

Ned was then taken into custody. Ben and the others watched him be taken under guard, but Knox assured Ben and Gill that he would later plead Ned's case privately before Schuyler to convince the general to give Ned the second chance he needed to redeem himself by rejoining the artillery train."

"I heard that, Colonel," said General Schuyler, taking Henry's hand and shaking it.

"Private Bottomly, sir, he's a good man at heart, misguided but—"

"He is a deserter, sir."

"No, not really. He only deserted out of confusion due to the chicanery of a major who abused his position, chicanery that this court, too, was all too willing to believe."

"And he was on his way to rejoin the army at Ticonderoga, sir," Gill added. "I'll swear to that."

"Me, too!" added Ben.

Schuyler ran his hand over his beard, then said, "He's under your command, Henry, and so I leave it to you to discipline your own man."

"Hard work will do that, sir, and we have a long, hard road ahead."

The general apologized for the entire incident and the loss of several days to Henry's timetable. "Unfortunately, there is no chance whatsoever of making it to Washington on New Year's Day. After all this is Sunday, New Year's Day!"

"We'll manage as best we can, General. Thank you for your help in the courtroom."

"Thank you, Henry, for exposing Pritchett for what he is."

"An ambitious man. He all along wanted to march into Washington's camp with *my* artillery train!" Then the general brightened and said, "You are all invited to dine with me for New Year's dinner tonight, at my mess hall here at the fort—and see to it that every member of your artillery train gets his fill!"

"Your hospitality is appreciated, and we will definitely take full advantage, sir, and sir…you knew the truth all along. I could tell by your demeanor during the proceedings, so why did you allow it to…to proceed at all?"

"Why to bring out Pritchett to take the bait. The trial was a snare."

"You might've told Henry that," William blurted out.

"Son, I had to have Pritchett believing himself to be winning. He had quite a file of half-truths stacked up against your brother, and I had to let out just enough rope for the man to hang himself."

"And if Ned had not been dragged back?" asked William.

"The chance I had to take. Every officer in my command had been poisoned against you, by then, I mean, Henry…I had to act."

"Thanks to the major," said Ben.

The general smiled at Ben and nodded. "Tonight then, six-thirty, seven…at the *mead hall*! But you, Henry Knox, I want to speak privately with you in my quarters, where we can speak our minds about the next plateau for your artillery train."

"Yes, sir. Thank you, sir."

"I will see you then."

CHAPTER FIFTEEN

The general was a man of his word. Every member of the Artillery Train had a turkey dinner awaiting them when they arrived at the mess hall. General Schuyler gave them a hearty personal welcome, and then he and Henry left, disappearing into the depths of the fort.

It was the following night, now the third night in Albany, and Henry was again dining with the general while his men had begun to move all the artillery across the frozen Hudson River, below General Schuyler's window where Henry stood watching the progress over the ice. The temperature had dropped, and once more the men were cut holes into the ice to allow the water below to bubble up and over, to form an ice bridge. It had become like a habit to do so with any river crossing, but here with the wide Hudson, they must take extra precautions indeed.

Knox watched the men at this work. Layer after layer of ice went into the building of the strongest bridge they could create of water and ice, until nightfall had descended. They had gotten most of the cannon across by now, but the heavy-laden sleds had taken their toll by cutting deep ruts into the ice where they had successively crossed over to the other side.

The tired, hungry, bleary-eyed, and surly men lacked sleep, but a cheer went up when the last cannon finally made it across. Henry turned from the window, his worry over the crossing having melted away at last. "I want to thank you, General, for rousing the locals to help us so much."

"I had that man Farley arrested. Turns out that he, too, was being pressured by Pritchett to increase his prices."

"I had such an argument with that man. Now it all makes sense."

The two military men had become fast friends over all the drama and obstacles that had been thrown in Knox's way. With worries set aside, Henry settled down to enjoy the sumptuous meal that the general was sharing with him.

At the site of the artillery, Ben and William walked the length of the ice bridge, returning across the river to check on a small sled filled with supplies and their own tents. Knox had left the pair along with Gill in charge, making it clear to Ben and Will that they had Henry's trust. Now, as they neared the Albany shore again, a large, black shape, sitting squarely among the trees, caught their eyes at the same instant.

"Ben, what is that?"

"Oh dear…oh my gosh, Will…it's Old Sow!"

"But we gave the signal! All the sleds are—*ahhh* were across the river! How'd she get back here?"

"Obviously, we were wrong!"

"How do we explain this to Henry?"

"How did we miss it? It's the size of two elephants."

"The oxen alone!"

202

"The fool oxen might have said something," Ben said attempting to make light of the situation they found themselves in.

"What're we to do? It's dark now, and you saw how deep the sled ruts have already cut into the ice."

"We'll have to have this sled straddle the ruts and keep atop the ice, Will."

"Maybe we should wait till daybreak, then. It'd give us time to do some more icing over."

"Where's Gill?"

"Gone off to bed already, he's exhausted."

"All right. We can do this, Will. We just have to not let the sled slip into one of those deep ruts out there on the ice."

Will nodded. "Let's do it before anyone's any the wiser."

"Wasn't Mr. Becker in charge of this sled?" asked Ben. "This is his fault, and he's just left it here among the trees."

"My pap's bad off sick," came a voice out of the darkness. It was Davey Becker. "He's caught that pneumonia that's been going around."

"According to whom?" Will angrily asked.

"According to the fort doctor. He's laid up something awful. I had to help him off the sled and over to the fort; I come back to take the sled across." Davey was the same age as Ben. Their eyes met in the dark here among the trees. "Good, then the three of us will see the Old Girl across."

"Right…come daybreak, nobody'll be any the wiser," added Will.

They shook on it, and then they went to work, Ben telling Davey, "Once you hit the ice road, stay out of the old ruts created by the other sleds. Make sure you stay on the topmost layer of ice. I'll burn a torch to light the way, and we'll walk the animals across."

"I'll toss chips at the oxen and chop ice anywhere it looks like we might need more," added Will.

"You fellas just relax. We already made two river crossings with the Sow in tow."

"A distinct warmer wind's been blowing down the valley all day, Davey," replied Ben.

"By morning, the ice may break apart," added Will. "We have to chance it now."

Davey climbed atop the sled, moving the oxen expertly out of the trees and to shore and the ice bridge. Ben had found an axe and handed it over to Will, saying, "If things should go wrong and that 44-pounder splits the ice, we have to cut the team loose, and fast." He held up the huge knife he kept in a scabbard, the whole of it a gift from Gill. He wished Gill was here with them now, but Gill had said he wanted to visit Ned in jail and then turn in.

"Go easy," Will told Davey. "Follow Ben's torch and lead."

"Will, stop your worrying."

"Take every precaution," replied Will.

"Carrying our axes and knives with us, well...you fellas aren't inspiring no confidence in me."

"We have every confidence in you, Davey," replied Ben, leading the oxen now out onto the ice, his lit torch helping him to guide the oxen so as to straddle the deep cut ruts.

All the other men of the train had long since turned in, all thinking they had completed the task of getting all the cannons across. How it came to pass that not a single one of them had noticed the notable Old Sow had not been led across from Albany, Ben was left to ponder.

"Get on there!" Ben prodded the oxen, yanking at the yoke via a cord of hemp he'd tied to it. "Come along, I tell you." He held out the torch ahead of him to light their way, but it was a moonless and starless night, so beyond the torch was only darkness.

Will encouraged the animals with a small whip and by tossing wood chips at their rumps as he had learned to do.

"Feels right solid to me," said Davey from his perch atop the sled, reins in hand.

"We're still in the shallows yet," replied Ben. "Keep your animals moving, no slow down."

"You mean, don't let a dumb animal lead you when you can lead it?" asked Davey with a slight laugh.

"Don't let them have an idea," replied Ben, using an expression the teamsters used often.

"You mean like picnicking on the ice?" joked Will.

"Can you see the ruts to avoid, Davey?" asked Ben.

"I see 'em, yeah." Davey said, then began to tell the other boys a story about how the oxen had decided to come to a complete stop in the dark right

205

at the cemetery as they were entering Albany a few days before. I kept hearing a moaning and grunting coming from the tombstones. Pap was getting rest, asleep in the back of the sled, and I could not get those animals out of there fast enough, but the two stubborn oxen refused to budge, and all along, I am hearing the ghosts in the cemetery calling me like a soft plea and moan."

"You just trying to scare us, Davey?"

"Not at all. This is a true story. The oxen had stopped cold and would not take another step, and as I was trying to pull them out of there, I fell over Tom Calder! Tom had fallen off the sled ahead of us, drunk as a skunk, and those oxen would not step on him. The ghostly sounds were coming from Tom all along!"

This had all three of the boys laughing, and Davey added, "The oxen had more sense than any of us that night."

Ben pictured the stubby, bald Tom Calder posing as a ghost there in the snowdrift, and how the oxen refused to stomp over him. He did not think the oxen should be mistaken for angels for drunks, but he and Gill had tried to get Henry to get rid of Calder as he was a danger to the train. Ben tucked the story away for when he might talk to Henry again about Tom Calder. Meanwhile, they had reached the center of the river when all three of the boys heard something like wood cracking. The sound was not loud, nor was it frightening in and of itself, but then the torch Ben carried picked up the thin, crooked line appearing between his feet, and it was not a grove or a rut made by earlier sleds going across.

Ben realized that the sled with Davey atop it had slipped into earlier ruts, and these deep grooves would not be easy to pull out of. The ice was thinnest in the ruts cut by the day's long crossings.

"Willian, Davey! The ice here's no good! Threatening to split open!" he shouted to the other two.

"I'm in the ruts, aren't I?" asked Davey.

"Can you get out of them is the question?" replied Ben.

"Get to the side, Davey!" Will shouted over them.

Davey pulled hard to one side and slapped his reins at the same time, and the sled with the huge 44-pounder inched over, then slipped back into the easy grooves, went up to the side again, and once again slipped back into the ruts for a third time. Will joined Davey in cracking the whip over the backs of the oxen, shouting at the animals to *pull, pull, pull.*

"Help me up here, Will, with the pull rope!" Ben pleaded, pleased to see Will rush to it and grab hold of the yoke line. With Davey attempting to right the sled out of the ruts, and with the other two pulling also in the same direction, the oxen slowly got the message and began to respond, finally pulling the sled out of the now dangerous, deep-set ruts, when again Ben heard the crackling of ice beneath them. He imagined the worst case scenario, and so he lifted his huge knife and ordered Will to cut the lines on his side. "We can't lose the oxen to the river! Cut them loose!"

207

Ben went for the lines with his knife, but Will was reluctant on his side to do so, saying, "Hold on! I think we're just past the fracture."

"Will's right, Ben! We're moving fast now for the shallows on the other side. We can make it!"

"Don't cut the lines!" added Will.

Ben realized that the tremors below his feet had subsided, as had the sound of cracking ice, when suddenly the sounds returned with a vengeance. "Davey, move fast for the shallows on the other shore, now!"

There was no more time or chance for a torch lit, careful procession. It was 'do or die' time now as the ice behind the sled began crumbling and breaking up. Will also shouted, "Move, Davey, as fast as you can for the other shore!"

Davey did his level best, but Ben could see the water chasing the sled runners. The ice behind them had opened up like a gaping wound, and it was coming for them—this mouth that wished to swallow them and the oxen whole. Ben could not get near the oxen to cut them loose now as the sled and animals had raced ahead of Will and him. They had to run for their own lives at this point, and men shore rushed out to help. The men who had pitched tents for the night, hearing the commotion, now rushed to the riverbank to determine the cause of the great noise welling up from the angry river now threatening to engulf the three young men, the oxen, and the Old Sow.

Ben and Will caught up to the sled which was now half sunken into the icy waters. "Cut the lines! Save the animals!" the boys shouted in unison while

208

they quickly whacked away at the tethers that held the animals in tow. As soon as the animals were cut free, the river finished off the sled and the cannon, sucking the 44-pounder into its muddy bottom. The oxen, too, would have slipped into the water with the lost cannon as well had Ben and Will not cut them loose. Even so, the freed animals stumbled, wobbled, stood, bawled in a most pitiable fashion, then fell again, only to slip and slide on the more solid ice of the shallows, until finally, they plodded to shore. Delighted it seemed at the reception from the men who'd prayed for their survival, the two brutes, still yoked to one another finally found *terra firma* to the cheers of the men who'd watched the drama unfold.

The icy waters had very nearly swallowed up Will, but Ben grabbed one end of the whip Will held onto, and he held this lifeline tight even as the hungry and growing eighteen-foot hole swallowed the sled and now the two boys. Only Davey had escaped going into the water, having leapt from the seat and run to shore.

Ben was aware that the Old Sow might well have sucked them under as it displaced water so rapidly. He was aware that either one of them or both could have been knocked unconscious against the metal, or that the frigid river itself might easily kill them. Fortunately, the Old Sow preferred to remain relatively upright. Like the smaller cannon that had been helped into the water at Sabbath Day Point, the barrel and much of the sled was sticking up at a forty-five degree angle from the shallows.

They had indeed nearly gotten the big gun across entirely, but no such luck.

Ben, holding fast to the whip, found some solid ice and climbed from the frigid river soaked and chilled to the bone, but all his attention was on Will. He tugged hard at the whip, feeling Will's tug back, so he began pulling at his end, finally seeing Will surface. Others came out to help the young men from the killing water, carrying blankets which they draped over the boys. They were then helped to shore amid a myriad of questions.

"Why didn't ya call for help?"

"Why didn't ya wait for daylight?"

"What were ya thinking anyways?"

While still shivering, teeth clacking from the cold, Will said to Ben, "H-H-Henry's go-going to-to be upset."

"Y-Y-Yeah…the Old Sow's his b-baby."

Henry had come immediately, straight from the general's quarters where he was having a brandy when he saw the torch and a few men struggling with a sled across the ice at night. It was hard to make out, but he feared the worst, that it was the Old Sow, and it had somehow missed getting across until now. He'd made a quick apology to the general and rushed out to the river. He'd had to go upriver a hundred or so yards to make his way around the broken ice, and by then, the Old Sow was well under the ice and in the shallows on the other side of the river, and two men had, from what he could see, gone into the frigid water as well. He got to the scene as the men, who turned out to be

William and Ben, were being thrown under blankets and led to warm fires. At this point, Henry was much more concerned to know if Ben and Will were all right more so than if the big artillery piece was all right.

When Henry stormed into the camp where the two boys shivered under blankets before a roaring fire, he repeatedly asked if they were all right. Most of the rest of the night was spent in telling the story of what happened from all viewpoints. The stories caused a good deal of laughter, but by daylight, seeing the condition of the Old Sow, no one was laughing any longer.

It also appeared that all of Albany had heard the news, as the river banks were lined with people who had come out to see for themselves the results of dropping a 44-pound cannon into the drink. The townspeople were so excited that it was an occasion for a party, it seemed. For Ben and Will, it seemed that they had all come out to laugh at them.

In actual fact, however, the entire town got behind the work of how to retrieve the Old Sow out of her predicament. No one wanted to see her left behind by the train, so the men of Albany came with their fresh teams, along with all manner of tools, hemp, block and tackle. They also willingly climbed into the water and put their backs into getting the monster cannon, and her now perpendicular sled back atop the ice so as to run it the rest of the way to shore. But this attempt proved futile, as each time they got it up onto the ice, the ice gave way again.

"I have a proposal, Colonel Knox," Ben said to Henry. "And I think it should work…in theory."

Henry gave Ben a dubious look; after all, it had been Ben who'd gotten them into this mess. "What is your *ahhh* theory, Ben?"

"If we were to break up all the ice between the cannon and the shore, since we built the sleds to act as floats, we ought to be able to float the big gun right to us using ropes to keep her steady, sir."

"By thunder, you've got it. That must work!"

Knox shouted out the plan, and every man went to work with axes and hammers, busting up a wide swath of the ice for the Old Sow to float without impediment. Allowing her weight and the sled to work in a floatation manner did the trick to the delight and roar of the crowd. They'd been held up by the accident, but not by many hours. Still, Knox wanted every Albany volunteer and cheering soul in the town to know something before he and the artillery train left for good.

Once he got everyone's attention and after much thanks to Albany for her hospitality, "Despite the military's attempt to court martial me—" This drew such laughter, Henry had to pause. "Despite some hardships like a 44-pounder in the Hudson muck, your fair city has been kind and generous to the men under my command and to me. For this reason, I am changing the name of this fat old cannon today to forever be known as The Albany!"

A huge cheer went up over this, and it echoed up and down the valley. The men of the train began a workman's song as they began to move out, and they continued to hear the cheers of the grateful people of Albany as they continued on their long journey.

Ben watched the men of the Knox Artillery train; they were reinvigorated as never before, and he realized that they had welcomed Ned Bottomly back into the fold with a spirit that said they were a proud unit and cared for one another as brothers on a mission should. For the first time on this incredible journey of three hundred miles, the artillery train was appreciated by the American townspeople in every hamlet they went through. It was a kind of reward, and it filled Ben and the other soldiers with pride, and a sense that they were making history.

The artillery train now moved more efficiently than ever, thanks to the Old Post Road out of Albany on January 5, 1776 than at any previous time. The road that ran between Albany and Kinderhook, was primarily used for the mail runs, and it was created by the British army years before. It certainly proved a blessing indeed for the artillery train. A true roadbed it was to everyone's delight, including the oxen. It was like a dream after what these men and beasts had traversed up till now.

As a result, the train was in and out of Kinderhook without stopping. It was four days later, January 9th when they stopped in Claverack—their last stopover in New York State. They'd come just over thirty miles from Albany in that time, and over one hundred and ten miles from Fort Ticonderoga.

Tired but confident, the Knox soldiers settled in for the night at Claverack for a much needed rest. Everyone knew that their next major effort would take them into the wilderness they all dreaded—the

Berkshire Mountains. They'd already seen the foothills, but it was now time to cut sharply eastward, straight through the thickest forest on their agenda, the one Knox had wisely sent Ned and Gill into in order to mark the fastest route from the Claverack region to the Massachusetts side of the mountains.

For now, in tiny Claverack Village, most of the men had nestled in at the smithy's shop and stables. There Ben bedded down alongside Gill and Ned. Gill said, "We'll be in the Greenwoods tomorrow, and Great Barrington…maybe…if we're lucky."

"Greenwoods?" asked Ben, weariness in his voice. "I don't recall seeing anyplace called that on the map."

Ned laughed. "No, it's not on any map, Ben."

"It's not a town, Ben," explained Gill. "That's just what the locals call the foothill region."

"Is there a road there?"

Again Ned laughed and this time Gill joined in. "Cart path, you might say," Gill finally said. "And even that'll be disappeared by time we arrive at the mountains."

"Thick forests, I hear."

"Thickest evergreen forest you'll ever see, son," Ned replied.

"Dark even by day," added Gill. "Pretty in a way, but you won't know it haulin' these cannons through it—not for her beauty, anyway."

The men fell silent, sleep seeping in, overtaking them, when Ben heard Gill share a chilling remark. "My father was one of three men who got trapped in

214

the Berkshires one winter, Ben, one of three, and all three froze to death."

Ben pulled his blanket tighter around himself, chilled at the thought.

"They were surveyors...doing a job."

"I'm sorry to hear it, Gill."

Ned had begun to snore, fast asleep.

"The Berkshires can kill a fool man quick, and my father, he was no fool, Ben. It can be treacherous those mountains. Why one good Nor'easter comes up, it could stop our artillery train cold—trap us amid the mountains till the spring thaw."

"Which could mean a terrible delay in getting the guns to General Washington."

"Exactly."

"Then...then why are we going that way?"

"It's the only way across."

"That's why you've been so restless lately, isn't it, Gill?"

Gill did not answer, instead saying, "Best we all get some sleep."

Ben felt as if all this time he had not known Gill, not by half. Ben's having heard how Gill's father had perished made Gill somehow more *like* Ben, an orphan. The only difference was that Benn had never known his own father. "Night Gill. And Gill, I hope we'll always be friends."

"Why not? Sure we will, Ben. Now, get some shuteye."

The following days were as grueling for the gun-haulers as Gill had warned. With each forward step, the dense forest closed in around the slender thread of cannon-bearing sleds and oxen. Gill had not exaggerated in his description. Daylight did not penetrate the thick canopy of green, and Ben learned quickly why this place was called Greenwoods. Everything was cast in green hues, even a man's skin. There existed here tall columns of hemlock, spruce, red, and Jack pine with the occasional white birch. The crews out ahead felling trees along the path marked by Gill and Ned were felling twice and thrice the trees of earlier treks to clear the path.

The maze of this tangled forest, the thickness of the undergrowth, the lack of civilization, it all conspired to make men want to turn and run. It declared of itself, there could never be a road or a clearing here that the forest could not retake. The bluffs, the precipices, and gullies framed by towering stone walls, outcroppings, and hanging boulders—granite or otherwise—alternated with deep chasms and steep slopes, until the train was forced to go back and around the mountain passes, sometimes requiring hours of forced teaming with nature to locate the best valley bottom or better crossing. Days were lost in this way.

Knox, still using Ben's mare, rode up and down the line, shouting, "Once we get shed of these mountains, boys...once we see Springfield on the other side, it'll be smooth going again. We'll have a real road to travel on once again. Don't be discouraged!"

"How far to Springfield, Gill?" Ben quietly asked. The two of them had been put in charge of the Old Sow, now called *The Albany*. They sat side-by-side on the sled seat, the oxen lazily pulling them along. Ben felt that the rocking motion was not unlike the bob and weave of a ship at sea.

"It's only thirty miles, Ben, but there's no straight line, so by the time we zigzag across these here mountains, you may's well call it sixty miles."

Ben groaned in response. "Longest thirty miles God ever made, eh?"

Gill laughed lightly. "You know what Ned and I marked as our best trail was long ago marked by others before us."

"Like your father?" Ben blurted out.

"Yes, sure…but before him and others of our kind, the Indians had trailed a footpath here, same as the Appalachian Trail."

"What Indians?"

"Indians of the Hudson Valley, they traded with one another. The Iroquois, the Mohawks, and the Algonquin-speaking Mohicans dwelling in the Connecticut River valley."

"I suppose the natives made the crossing look easy, huh?"

"Well now, they weren't dragging cannons with them, or fending off saboteurs, or dealing with stubborn oxen!"

Except for a place Great Barrington, no larger than a handful of shacks, the artillery train had seen nothing of others for the last forty miles. Meanwhile, every hour, Knox consulted with Ned and Gill, sending out Ned ahead of the train to scout out markers that he and Gill had notched in trees and report back. The best compass failed to be accurate in this region.

When Knox and Ben had both asked why compasses did not work well here, Ben replied, "The spirit of the mountain doesn't care for such contraptions of mankind." Then he added, "How should I know?" His shrug added to the moment.

Waterfalls announced themselves before they were seen, and despite the cold and huge frozen sections framing the water, they flowed freely. They came upon small ravines a man could step over, but before long the ravine became a pond ahead of them, and the pond turned into a lake with a falls and a chasm, and at the bottom of such chasms, the water became a full-blown river.

When they stopped on a ridge fronting one such river to build fires and rest for the night, Colonel Knox found Ben and Gill at their section of the train. Together with Will and Ned listening in, Knox conferring with them about the morale of the men, which again had taken a bad turn, thanks to the obstacles of the Berkshires.

"You were right, Ned, Gill...about this place. You sure warned me."

"I got a feeling in my bones, too, sir...about a coming snowfall."

"We could use a little snow for the sleds," he replied.

"Not too much, sir...not in these parts," said Gill. "Could cost us all dearly."

"I haven't seen any evidence of a storm brewing," said Ben.

"Ben...when is the last time you saw the sky?" asked Gill.

Ben shrugged. "Since before we entered the forest here."

"Exactly."

Ned piped in with, "You can't see it coming here; you have to smell it and feel it."

"These mountains are funny," added Gill. "For all we know, it could be snowy in the next valley over right now, and we'd never know it."

"Funny," repeated Knox, sipping at his hot coffee. "I'm learning that fast. Snow cover is too thin where we're at. Making the work twice as hard on the oxen."

"Without snow, the skids are as useless as broken wagon wheels," said Ben. "If no snow at all, the sleds would do better on wheels."

"Mother Nature has tested us the entire way, men. If you recall, we had so much snow when approaching Albany that we could hardly move in it. Now not enough and a threat of too much at once!"

"Same at Saratoga," added Will.

"We may have to fashion wheels for the sleds if...if," began Knox, "if Westfield up ahead has a blacksmith shop and the materials."

"Maybe we can find men willing to sell us wagons," suggested Ben.

"Two problems with that, Ben. One, do such men and wagons exist, and if so, how do we pay for them? Our funds are exhausted."

"And as we've seen along the way, some men are interested only in coin," said Gill.

"What if…what if," stuttered Ned.

"Go on, Ned," Knox encouraged him.

"What if Major Pritchett paid our way the rest of the trip?"

"How is that?" Knox and the others stared at Ned.

"I hid away the sack of coins he gave me to…to be his spy. I didn't feel right taking it, not in the end, so I hid it where I thought Ben here would find it."

"Where's that?" asked Gill.

"The Little Sow—down her barrel."

"Well now…surely Major Pritchett wanted to contribute to the cause all along," Knox replied, smiling. The others broke out in laughter as Ben went to the cannon and discovered the sack of coins and snatched it from the breach, holding it up to the cheers of the others.

Ben Cross awakened the next morning in his tent with the fresh aroma of a new snowfall filling his senses; as if by magic, the moment he opened his eyes, he knew that Gill's prediction for snow had come true. They needed the snow at this juncture, as it had become so scarce that the skids had become an impediment to forward movement, and the oxen again and again slowed to a standstill due to the resistance to they felt in trying to pull their precious cargo over rocky ground. Ned warned that the earth here grew a fresh crop of stones every season, and from all appearances, he'd not lied on that score.

Ben heard men up and down the line shouting the single word that he wanted to shout: *Snow!* Although not a large snowfall, it was enough to excite everyone, as it would ease the load for the oxen. The caravan quickly began to move forward, but only after Ben and others ate a rushed breakfast. They were now moving due east, headed for the town of Blanford—western Massachusetts and Gill's home town where his father's remains and those of his mother rested in the cemetery. "Mind you now, when they passed away, there was no town there…only a handful of families and the cemetery," Gill had said at the campfire the previous night, when everyone was swapping out stories.

From Blanford, according to the maps Ben had seen, they would target the larger town of Westfield—*which was on the maps*, and from there, they would finally be back to Springfield, Massachusetts, but the Berkshires still stood in their way. This particular area of the Berkshires felt like another planet to Ben—another world than any he had known growing up in Boston. It stood in stark contrast to the land and forests of coastal towns, yet it was a part of the colony where fiercely independent men had left their remote homes to fight and defend Bunker Hill and now Cambridge and Boston.

Seven miles later, they stumbled on a place not on the map, a tiny village of homesteader called Otis, deep in the mountains. They moved on as the mountain people stood about in total shock and amazement to see the caravan pass by them. *Quite the parade for these folks*, Ben thought, waving to the children who were waving at him, huge grins on each face.

Beyond Otis, and even before they found sleepy Westfield, Ned, scouting ahead and east of Westfield, located a bridle path. It was not much, but it was something to follow; this welcomed cow path, like the new fallen snow in just the right amount, promised to ease their burden even if just a little. When the caravan actually reached Westfield, the cannoneers heard a strange noise that boomed and trumpeted down the valley walls, and as they neared the town, they found themselves being greeted by a small band, the instruments battered and ancient, but the musicians were full of what Gill called "piss and vinegar"—enthusiasm for their rendition of a number of songs of patriotism and gaiety. News of the Knox Train had been spread by their scout, Ned, and so the locals had gotten up this band to serenade Colonel Knox and his band of patriots. This really made a parade of things!

A banner which read **WELCOME** in bold letters had been strung across Main Street. Some of the local women offered up dippers of water, and many had baked pies and cakes and insisted the soldiers of the Knox Train take them, and many of the local men insisted on spelling the drivers for several miles the other side of town. The man who introduced himself as "The fellow everyone around here calls the mayor" shook Knox's hand and offered him the key to the city, a wooden token.

"Honestly, we've never had a single cannon ever come through Westfield, sir," the mayor informed Knox.

"And now look!" added the mayor's wife. "We've got so many coming down Main Street at once!"

The men, women, and children of Westfield came in closer and, as each cannon passed by, and soon they were standing close enough to do what they wanted—to touch the cannons as they passed. When The Albany, formerly The Old Sow, passed, the townspeople stared in awe, altogether amazed at her sheer size. Ben heard people saying, "I never knew they made a cannon this large."

The train stopped long enough east of town for the men to partake of the drinks and cakes as well as the hospitality and good cheer. Ben found himself explaining to a group of young boys the names of each type of cannon and how each was unique. It made him feel like a school teacher with the small mob gathered about him under a tree. The gun-haulers and teamsters were amused and pleased at the sudden attention, and Gill said, "It's like Albany all over again *without* the court martial!"

Things had settled and quieted too much, so the mayor shouted at the band to "Strike up the music!" His wife then told Knox, "We've arranged for cider and ale barrels at the general store for you and your men, Colonel."

On hearing this, the Knox men cheered in unison, most making a beeline for the store and inn. The local innkeeper raised his hands and shouted, "We wish to show our patriotism and appreciation

223

for you men! I have whiskey for those who have the stomach for sour mash."

This sent up an even louder roaring cheer from the hearty soldiers. Meanwhile, Ben and Will continued to conduct 'class', explaining the measurements and caliber of each gun and howitzer.

One local asked Gill, "How's it possible, McCleary, to come over from Claverack alone hauling all this...this tonnage? Much less from Fort Ticonderoga!"

"It's been difficult, Samuel. I won't sugar-coat it. It's been...tedious, complicated, bone-wearying hard, but these men are determined."

A little girl asked Ben what the big handles on the side of each barrel were for, and he said for carrying, transport, "But they are called trunnions."

"Onions?"

"No, trunnions."

She replied, "No, I don't want no onions." The child ran to her mother, whispered in mom's ear, and hid behind her skirt, smiling and peeking out. Meanwhile, more questions rained down on Ben, Will, and Gill. Too many to handle in fact. This went on for nearly an hour, before Knox decided it was time to reward Westfield and its people with a great goodbye from their largest cannon—The Albany. He ordered Gill to oversee the reassembly of the Old Sow in order to fire her for Westfield as a thank you, and "To see what kind of a noise she will make!"

This took everyone by surprise, but then Henry Knox was full of surprises. "It's the least we can do!" he told the mayor and his wife, the innkeeper

224

and townspeople. "For your hospitality and patriotism."

When the Old Sow was assembled, she was magnificent and not nearly so sad looking as when broken down. When the ball was placed in her barrel, the fuse lighted, the trajectory to take the ball out into the wilds, everyone watched in rapt attention. When the powder was touched off, sparks flying, gasps preceded the enormous explosive shot, the noise deafening and followed by a roar of cheers and clapping.

The fireworks, however, did not satisfy one man among them, and since he was in charge, he ordered up a howitzer and a mortar with rounds, and he demonstrated how these smaller pieces of artillery were used in combating the enemy. The crowd and the Knox men, everyone loved the show of force and appreciated Henry's magnetic enthusiasm for the guns.

At one point, Henry began to teach the crowd on the use of a gunner's quadrant, holding one up over their heads, saying, "It shows the elevation by use of a simple arch. My men will adjust the barrel to the proper angle once I have made my calculations of distance and velocity, you see. The device looked like a simple square edge that any carpenter might use, Ben thought. Beside Henry, Ned jammed a long rod down the barrel, swabbing it clean. At the end of the rod was a gnarled metal brush like that used by a chimney sweep, but this head was twisted to scrape out all loose particles. A second man, Effram, plunged a sheepskin sponge on the end of a rod, completing the cleaning. Finally,

225

Gill handed Ned a bag of gunpowder and this was rammed into the barrel. Only then did Gill drop the cannonball down the muzzle. It was rammed home tightly against the gunpowder.

This demonstration complete, the barrel was elevated to the degree that Knox had calculated. He wished to strike a boulder far away in a cleft valley before them. As the men elevated the barrel to the degree requested, Henry spoke to the crowd. "We next take this long brass pick and slip it into a hole where the gunpowder bag is pricked open. The hole also acts as a necessary vent for the wick. Corporal McCleary, would you, sir, do the honors?"

Gill slipped a linstock, a long match-like stick with a gunpowder core into the vent, and when Knox was certain of the elevation, he shouted, "Fire!"

Gill lit the linstock fuse which flared like a 4th of July candle, and within seconds, the Old Sow fired her second shot, this time at a select target. Before the amazed eyes of the crowd, the boulder was exploded into countless pieces with the impact of the wrought iron ball. Cheers went up from everyone. For the children in particular, it was as if Henry might be Merlin the Magician from ancient books. The adults were thunderstruck at the power of The Albany. The biggest kid at the show was Henry.

The sound of the cannon rolled down the valley, and while deer, quail, and all manner of other animals were sent scurrying, the absolute silence after the blast felt more deafening than the blast itself. It was Ben who broke that silence,

226

shouting, "The Red Coats will hear that clear to Boston!"

Everyone laughed at the notion.

"Ben's right," defended Gill. "When the British do hear The Albany, and see her power along with our entire train, they'll pack up and be on their way home!"

This had become now a three hour layover and celebration, and darkness was descending, and as everyone in town was offering lodging for the soldiers, making it easy to say no to moving out this evening. About this time, some of the soldiers had downed enough spirits to begin to tell young ladies in the crowd that *they* would be happy to reassemble one of the cannons to fire it off expressly for the lady in question and just for the fun of it. Of course, they had no such magical powers or authorization. Still, Ben understood their enjoyment of the attention after all they had been through. Ben had himself been attracted to one young lady in the crowd, and he had been exchanging a series of flirtatious smiles and winks with her.

The Westfield welcome had brought cheer to the entire train, and by now, it was clear that every man on the train was seen as a hero. Everyone along their trail had learned of the hardships, often exaggerated by the storyteller, and everyone had gotten a detailed account of how they almost lost The Old Sow to the Hudson, and how it had gotten its new name, The Albany.

The celebration put Knox and the leaders of the town, including all of the officers of the Springfield Committee of Safety, who had heard how near the

227

artillery train was to Springfield and so had all come to greet Knox and his men here. They all sat at a table in the inn with Knox and the mayor and the innkeeper well into the night, all lifting glasses of ale and grog. Toast after toast was made to the success of getting the artillery this far so fast. The Springfield Safety Committeemen promised Knox that he and his men would get an even greater welcome in their city.

At daybreak the following morning, Henry and a lot of other hung over men had thought they might slip out while the town slept, but it was not to be. The entire town again turned out to see them off, so the train left Westfield to clapping and cheers that now felt like a nail in the brain of most of the teamsters, the soldiers, and the officers. Ben and Will, along with Davey had managed to sneak in some ale, but not so much as to be affected by a hangover like Gill, Ned, and Henry.

So much appreciation for them made the men of the train feel as if there was nothing they could not accomplish. Ben felt it as much as anyone, felt that there was no obstacle large enough to stop or slow their progress ever again. In fact, going out of Westfield, eastward bound, the caravan found itself moving more swiftly and smoothly than at any time since entering the dreaded Berkshires, thanks in large part to the welcome, the cakes, the clapping, and the local footpath, which was well cleared.

CHAPTER SIXTEEN

It was true; Springfield's welcome of the cannoneers proved to be greater than any previous party thrown for the patriots. Greater and more gracious, than Albany and Westfield combined, Ben thought. Colonel Knox had no choice but to find a sled to stand on and give a speech of thanks to the welcoming crowd, but this time, it was combined with a recruiting effort! He asked for volunteers, for all the New York men who were not his Cambridge soldiers, all who had volunteered from Ticonderoga to this point, were sorely in need of relief and the opportunity to return to their homes and families. There proved no lack of new volunteers in Springfield, and so many a goodbye was being said for the rest of the day as New York volunteers waved and began the long trek back—minus the back-breaking work.

Again Knox was moved to give the cheering crowd a demonstration of the power of the Old Sow, careful to call it The Albany, despite how the men kept chanting her original name. The celebrations, food, wine, ale, and camaraderie went on late into the night, but Knox assured every man that at daybreak, they would be pushing on toward their final destination without hesitation.

As Henry was a man who kept his word, he did not allow any dalliance the next day, and the train was waving goodbye to all of Springfield, save those who'd joined the train as new volunteers.

With the Berkshire Mountains behind them, the relatively flat, civilized forty miles between Springfield and Worcester, Massachusetts, brought on no delays! It was the first stretch of territory between towns and cities that had not brought on some delay or other. At Worcester, news of their approach heralded by their scout, Ned Bottomly, had gotten around to the point that many Worcester men now rode out to greet them miles before they reached the small city. On reaching the outskirts of town, Knox again saw that the street was strung with a huge welcoming banner and that the crowds had gathered.

Henry, Will, and Ben were also surprised to see a familiar face in the crowd, a pretty young woman, waving and shouting Henry's name. It was Lucy Knox, and Henry dismounted and ran into her arms. Their kiss and embrace brought up a cheer among the cannoneers and the townspeople at once.

Ox drawn sled after sled, piled high with the disassembled cannons passed beneath the welcome banner, going for the other end of town. All the men were enjoying yet another 'parade' and show of the big guns for the men, women, and children of Worcester. As Ben and the others moved down Main Street, they were offered pewter cups of ale, muffins, cakes, and near the outskirts the other side of town, they came upon a large carnival of tables filled with food and drink. Ben felt like a king coming back from the crusades being welcomed by his people. He had read all of the tales of the Round Table. He felt like a knight in some old-fashioned book by Sir Walter Raleigh.

The mayor of Worcester shouted everyone to silence, and once he got it, he gave a short speech praising Colonel Knox and all his 'gallant' men, ending with, "Our citizens offer you this feast in the hope that it grants you some small measure of our devotion and appreciation to your mission!"

When the backslapping and festivities on the common settled into calm, and after Ben finished his finest meal in days, he saw Lucy Knox, followed by her mother and father, the Whitakers, making their way through the crowd to get at Henry. Lucy carried a large box with a huge bow and ribbon—a belated Christmas present, and the Lucy's mother carried a smaller box also garlanded with ribbon and bow. Seeing this procession and Henry's reaction, everyone fell silent, watching, curious.

"Take it, Henry!" Lucy said, as she pushed the big box into this hands. "It's your coming home gift!" Lucy's eyes were filled with the light of joy.

Mrs. Whitaker, Henry's mother-in-law, scolded him. "Go on, Colonel! Open it!"

Knox tore away the ribbon, bow, and wrapping, opening the box and staring into its contents, his eyes going wide. He appeared speechless for the first time that Ben had known him. "Well show everyone what it is!" shouted Mr. Whitaker.

Knox lifted out a uniform of blue and buff colors very like the one Washington wore; it was jacket first, pants below. Henry fingered the gold buttons, ran his hand along the pleats and the insignia stitched onto the shoulders, the image of a cannon. The coat was faced and lined with scarlet and white loops of lace to fasten down the buttons

231

along the breast. "It's...it is beautiful," he finally said.

"Well, put it on!" Lucy insisted. "I must see if I got your fit right."

"You fashioned this by your own hand, Lucy?"

"I did."

Mr. Whitaker proudly said, "This uniform, Henry, was approved by General Washington himself expressly for your artillery regiment."

"Your entire regiment will be wearing the same colors, Henry," added Lucy, her smile infectious.

"So now..." began a stunned Knox, "you haven't sat idle all these many months while I was away!"

"No, I have been busy procuring ladies to help fashion your regimental garb!"

"Not to mention the materials," added Mrs. Whitaker, holding out the smaller box to Henry now. She said to Will. "Your gifts, Will are under our tree at home waiting for you!"

Ben felt a wave of sadness come over him. He had no home to speak of save Gray's shipyard. He wondered how much of it was left, how much burned for camp fires. He wondered how Mr. Gray, his mentor, and Ben's best friend Wilbur, were doing these many months.

Knox tore open the second box to reveal a Naval-styled hat to compliment the uniform, one befitting a man of his rank. Cheers went up among the revelers. Knox placed it onto his head to louder cheers and toasts all round.

"Now you look like a colonel in this man's army, sir!" Gill McCleary shouted and downed his ale to the final clapping and cheering, while Ben slipped away, wanting to be alone with his thoughts, weary, and seeking a warm place to sleep, perhaps a stable.

Will rushed to catch him, and said, "Wait up, Ben. I have something for you."

"What's that, Will?"

"Been carving it for some time. A gift."

Ben stopped in his tracks and stared at the small offering, a flute that Will had fashioned for him. "For me?"

"For you."

Ben blew into the flute. "It's got a perfect pitch."

"Where're you heading?"

"Off to find a straw bed; I am bone tired and sleepy."

"But Lucy and her parents want us to stay with them tonight. They have plenty of room and a bed for you and I to share."

"A bed? A real bed?"

"Come along!"

Ben needed no second telling, following Will back to the festivities.

The following day at noon of January 24th 1776, the Knox Artillery Train easily made the twenty miles to Framingham, which meant they were now within fifteen miles of Cambridge. Taking stock, however, Knox, with Ben at his side, found problems. Some of the sleds were in terrible repair as they had now been dragged not over snow but over rough roads bare of snow. Some had made the trip all the way from Fort Ticonderoga, while others had been fashioned or purchased at Fort George, later Albany. By now, some of the sleds had been discarded in dumps and trash heaps in towns like Worcester, replaced, by loading the cannon onto wagons, as wheels were needed now. At this point the artillery train was made up partially of wagons, but they didn't have enough of them for every cannon to be transported any further.

"We'll leave the train here, Ben, and go into Cambridge on horseback to confer with General Washington. Once there, we'll just confiscate the wagons we need, return and fetch the guns."

Ben nodded. "Sounds like a good plan."

"Then, my young friend, it's onward to finally deliver the artillery into General Washington's hands at Cambridge."

Ben realized it was the only sound plan, as many of the sleds would not make it another mile. By horseback, Knox, Ben, and Will rode into the Continental Army camp at Cambridge to find a dispirited army and a starving one as well. The months of waiting and holding the British at bay at the Bay of Boston had taken a great toll on Washington's troops. Still, Knox was pleased to see that those who had strength enough and morale enough were going through daily drills. However, Cambridge was flooded in places, much of the ground covered with deep mud, the result of early rains in an unusual year for weather. There were scattered patches of snow, but not enough for a rabbit to hide in. Since they had departed for Ticonderoga, several thousand more soldiers had joined the ranks of this determined army, which made for a terrible shortage of food, water, and ammunition. The volunteers dotted the land so tightly that it was difficult for Henry, Ben, and Will to get through on horseback. Soldiers of the Continental Army, who were not in tents, makeshift hovels, and lean-to's against trees, filled every stable, barn, and nearby farmstead.

"*Appears* that we still have a city to emancipate," Knox said to Ben and Will, speaking of Boston, when some private among the soldiers recognized Knox in his uniform and shouted the news that he was back. The word spread like wildfire throughout the camps, and as they managed to get to Washington's headquarters and dismount, the noise and cheering brought General Washington out of his office to greet them.

There was a surliness in many of the crowd gathering around, some asking, "Where are the big guns we keep hearing about?"

One fellow in tattered homespun clothes remarked on Colonel Knox's uniform, saying, "Will you *look-see-here* at the finery on this one?"

"Sure does look pretty," added another American soldier.

A sergeant shouted for respect of the rank, and Ben shouted, "Colonel Knox is the first man to wear the colors of the First Artillery Regiment in the American Army, and it's fitting that he should!"

A cheer went up among most of the men at this comment. Ben recognized how demoralized the majority had become since their leaving this place the previous fall. The image of a mob flitted through Ben's head, yet these were the men of the Continental Army! Dissident men who were bone-weary of inactivity, lack of food, clothing, and absolutely no pay as the Continental Army had no funds, and so no way to pay these men. Little wonder there had been word of rampant desertion from Washington's ranks. So much had conspired to work against the grand revolution. Deep gloom came from the sunken eyes of so many men now staring at Ben, Will, and Knox, no doubt wondering how they could possibly be looking so fit and chipper after their three-hundred mile trek with cannon in tow. The gloom they saw in the eyes also seemed to have settled over the entire camp like an invisible fog.

"Where are the guns!" another repeated."

"I don't see any artillery!"

Knox stood on his stirrups, giving the big man an even more larger-than-life appearance than normal. "The guns are at a safe location, but I am here to report to my commander-in-chief, after which General Washington will report, no doubt to his officers, who in turn will speak with all of you." Knox, his head held high, glared at the mob, then got down from his mount, and stepped up to Washington. The two tall men saluted one another, but then Washington embraced Knox before shouting to the soldiers present, "We all owe a huge debt of gratitude to this man and his regiment!"

Knox waved down the cheering throng, saying, "I won't be satisfied or serenaded until every artillery piece is deployed and in place at Roxbury, Charleston, and Dorchester!"

This heartened the soldiers who raised another round of cheers, to which Washington, shouting them down, added, "In due time, Colonel, I know you will see to it. You and your men have done the impossible, Henry."

"Very near impossible, but we pulled it off."

"And in doing so, you've accomplished a great service to your country."

Washington then addressed the men directly. "Every man here is needed now at the fortifications to protect the artillery where each cannon and mortar will be deployed. See your company lieutenants and sergeants for your detail."

The crowd disbanded with a renewed spirit, doing as Washington said. Ben and Will joined Knox at General Washington's side. "Colonel," began Washington, "you've given this camp and these men a renewed sense of mission, and that is something to cheer about. I want you and your two best men here to join me inside for a toast and a meal. A meager meal to be sure, but a meal nonetheless."

"I am honored, sir. Lead the way." Knox, Will, and Ben followed Washington through the double doors and down the corridor on a walk of pride.

Inside, they were treated to ale to quench their thirsts, and Knox explained the situation and circumstance with the guns left in Framingham. "Broke down parade, you might call it," said Knox.

"Left in Gill McCleary's care," added Ben, "but the corporal, he's got no way to make wagons materialize out of thin air."

"We'll get you the rest of the way, Ben," Washington said in reply. "We'll find the necessary number of wagons and get those guns in place overnight, even if we have to make two trips to Framingham to do so."

Knox, a note of anxiety in his voice, asked, "What of the British in Boston, sir? Are they as firmly entrenched as when we left?"

"Holding tenaciously to every inch and corner of the city and harbor, yes."

"And the latest intelligence reports, sir?"

"They say there are 17,000 civilians in the city; likely a conservative estimate."

Ben thought how his friend Wilbur was one of that number, still trapped in Boston.

Washington added, "900 of those civilians are estimated to be Tories, content to have the British guard on hand to smash the rabble—which would be us."

"And what of troop buildup, sir?"

"Pretty much the same—13,000 of King George's Regulars. They truly believe they have more than enough to swat this annoying fly and crush us come the next pitched battle."

"Is there no good news coming out of the colonies elsewhere?" Henry drained his ale.

"Our privateers like the Finn Hawk have cut off any chance for the Red Coats to receive any additional supplies," replied Washington. "We both know what that means."

"An army moves on its belly, yes."

"Then the British soldiers are going hungry, correct?" asked Ben.

Ben had been giving thought again to Wilbur and Mr. Gray's plight when he heard Washington's remark about the Finn Hawk, and the thought of her captain and crew cutting off shipping supplies sounded so swashbuckling to Ben that he wished he could be on board, when next they waylaid a supply ship on route to Boston.

"As far as our forces here stand, Henry," continued Washington, annoyed at some irritation to his gums or teeth, Ben could not be sure—"while they are eating fairly well, the men now number 14,000 at last count. Although we have lost a number of men to desertion, but far more have been lost to time!"

"Time?" asked Ben, confused

"Enlistment, time being up on their enlistments."

"*Ahhh*, I see," Knox answered for them. "My fault...my fault entirely."

"Not at all! How can you even say such a thing, Henry?" Washington was shaking head adamantly.

"Had we not lost so much time in Albany—held up there on—"

"On trumped up charges, I know! None of it anything you could have controlled. Now, I will not stand for any further such nonsense from you. No one could have delivered the Guns of Ticonderoga to Cambridge except Colonel Henry Knox."

Ben and Will cheered this remark and drained their glasses, and Washington added, "And as just payment, Henry, I've readied an artillery unit of six hundred men who will be under your direct command, sir!"

239

Knox was caught off guard, his eyes wide. "I-I-I don't know what to say, General."

"Say thank you, say I accept, just say something. I've never known you to be speechless, Henry." Washington gave out with a hearty laugh.

Knox looked long into Washington bright, intelligent eyes, a smile coming over Henry. "I will take command of my regiment immediately."

"And your first order of business?"

"Get the guns deployed and in place here!"

"Some other good news I hinted of—the British brigantine, *Nancy*, has been captured by your old acquaintance Captain Blaylock, and I am told that the *Nancy's* stores contains something of interest to our artillery plans."

"Munitions?" Knox was gasping at this news.

"Three thousand round shot for your 24-pounders, Henry!"

"I've more good news just sent me, Henry. News you will welcome."

"And what might that be, sir?"

Washington smiled wide. "Your old friend, Captain Blaylock has been made a vice admiral in the Continental Navy."

"Here I'd thought Captain Blaylock far out to sea by now," said Ben with a shake of his head.

"We pressed the Finn Hawk and her captain into service, Ben," replied Washington.

"Blaylock privately told me that he'd get us that much needed ammunition one way or the other," began Henry, grinning. "He hinted at the old way of the pirates, and it seems that he wasn't exaggerating after all."

Everyone laughed and raised their tin cups at this, and Washington said, "The kind generosity of the Nancy also gave up 10,500 flints, 2,000 muskets, and thirty tons of musket shot!"

Another cheer went up for these numbers.

Just before leaving to return to Framingham to load all the cannons onto the necessary wagons that Knox had gathered to his cause, Henry pulled forth an envelope that he handed to General Washington, where the general stood to wave them off outside his Cambridge headquarters.

"And what is this?" asked Washington, with a hint of curiosity.

"A small matter that you need not concern yourself with—until *after* we win the war that is, sir."

"*Ahh*...the small matter of your reimbursement for out of pocket costs. Leave your bill with me, and I do so appreciate your financing this entire effort, Henry."

"I am only sorry that the bill is more than twice what I had originally calculated it would be, but in these times," began Knox in an apologetic tone, but Washington brushed his apology off with a wave of his large hands.

"Henry," Washington solemnly said as he read the damages, "two thousand, three-hundred dollars is a small price to pay for Boston."

241

CHAPTER SEVENTEEN

Wishing to take full advantage of the Ticonderoga guns, General Washington ordered the artillery be brought from Framingham and deployed at key positions all around the city of Boston. He wanted this work done in complete silence and by cover of darkness, so to in no way alert the enemy to the fact that the Continentals now possessed artillery.

In broad daylight, however, the general had men working on fortifications and earthworks, and he even had a sturdy, one-hundred bed hospital constructed in the field—all within sight of the British—which construction covered the business of providing for the cannons.

Washington wished for the British to believe he was preparing for an all-out assault across Boston Neck—which would be a suicidal act. Attacking via the only avenue into the city is precisely what the Red Coats wanted him to do.

Meanwhile, Knox and his men brought on the cannons, but the order had gone out that there must be no cheering or hoopla…nothing to alert British guards down at the city gates. Knox, on his return, oversaw the work of finishing the fortifications and earthworks by day, and the moving of the guns into position by night.

Gill, now a sergeant of artillery, worked alongside Knox, as did Ned, along with Private William Knox and Private Benjamin Cross.

During the same days, which stretched into weeks, the siege *appeared* to remain a stalemate, but in truth a steady, silent stream of American soldiers labored on the leeside of Dorchester Heights. The soldiers worked in silence like so many hundreds of monks. Using well-greased, oxen-drawn wagons, and equally well-greased draglines, block and tackle, the work went on under the noses of the Red Coats. While they were merely across the bay, just south of Boston, the hills kept them from sight of anyone in the city. Henry pointed out to Ben how the Heights made for the ideal location for the field pieces, well within range.

The men, most of whom had not worked with artillery, worked with a kind of fevered pride. Ben and William had long held this pride of the guns, a feeling that Henry had passed on to them, but now it welled up in the young men to see the guns being dragged the final few feet and locked into position, their barrels directed and leveled on the British and their ships in Boston, Harbor.

Days and days had been taken up with training, as most of the soldiers had never seen a cannon, before, much less worked with artillery. Many others had been put to the hard labor of creating the breastworks. Both Knox and Washington fully expected and feared that the British would learn what was going on and charge them before they were ready. It certainly would happen once the big guns opened up. For this reason, entrenching tools, timber, barrels, hay bales, powder, and muskets— all the way from the Finn Hawk—were now on hand. Charleston, Cobble Hill, the Flatlands before Cambridge, Roxsbury, and Dorchester.

It was now a moonless night this March 2, 1776 and the bombardment would begin at dawn, but not before four hundred oxen and two thousand men worked through the night to raise two new forts on Dorchester Heights. From here, Knox would command the Old Sow and the 24-pounders.

Moments before sunrise, the big guns were revealed when a screen of sandbags, barrels, and bundles of wood was torn down by the Continental soldiers. All this time, the Red Coats failed to detect or suspect a thing.

Henry took personal command of the Old Sow, of course, and oversaw the 24-pounders as well. Moments before sunrise, Henry shouted, "We're going to see history made today, men!" He stopped before Ben, William, and Gill, all of whom stood together. "We've come a long, long journey together, my friends, my brothers in arms."

Gill nodded and said, "What do you and the general think will happen when we open fire on 'em, Colonel?"

Knox pursed his lips, scrunched his features in thought, and confessed, "Frankly, Gill, I can't predict what'll come of our attack, other than to say, it will come as a shock."

"But you do believe we've fooled them completely," said William.

"They still think the guns captured at Fort Ticonderoga are three hundred miles northwest of here, don't they?" asked Ben.

"Yes—why, if they knew we had the guns here, they'd have stormed us long before now. They'd want to disrupt any chance we'd have of properly training the men on how to deploy and properly fire the guns."

"Then there's a fair chance that the war could be over tomorrow?" asked Will, his eyes alight with the thought. "I mean if we beat them and they go running off, we'll have won!"

"The battle for Boston, perhaps, we will win," said Knox, now that we have the guns to do so. But the war itself, that will drag on, Will."

"It's sure to be a victory," said Ben.

"Ben, I love your optimism," replied Knox. "Your faith in all things, and your desire for all to be well. Yes, boys, the American Ox will beat back the British Lion today, here at Boston, but the end of the Boston Siege while a blow to the Red Coats, will not end their aggression toward us."

"Ain't today the sixth anniversary of the Boston Massacre?" asked Gill.

"Why, to be sure…yes! Yes it is." Knox said as he slapped Gill on the back. "When we retake Boston," added Knox in firm determination, "the British will certainly know one thing."

"What's that?" asked Ben and Will in unison.

"We Americans mean business! We mean to stand up for our rights!"

Ben nodded and asked, "How long do you think the war will go on, Colonel?"

General Washington appeared as if from thin air, and upon hearing Ben's question, he cleared his throat. All of them came to attention as Washington

245

replied to Ben, saying, "No one can answer your question, Ben." Washington's voice had a melancholy tone to it, here in the fog of morning with the sunlight creating a thin grayness, the color of the cannon, over the horizon. "No one, not even my confident, young Colonel Knox."

"Have you come to inspect the fortifications, sir?" asked Knox.

"Yes, along with the placement of the cannons, but mostly to be on hand when the First American Artillery unit fires on those British ships. They'll want to protect their ships. If we are lucky, they'll board and retreat to save their naval vessels."

It was an important time, Ben realized, and he felt a sense of great pride swelling up within him, in being here with Knox and Washington, on the cusp of history.

When the first solid rays of the sun stretched across the Atlantic and touched Boston Harbor, Knox ordered the cannoneers to wait for the sun to caress the cannons with its kiss and blessings where they stood at fortifications on Dorchester Heights. The muzzles and barrels had all been polished, and they now reflected like mirrors. They were already raised and pointed on the British position, and this was the first glimpse that the Red Coats, looking through their field glasses, had of the Guns of Ticonderoga. In this instance, any spy system they may have had, simply had failed the British.

General George Washington, riding his white steed, shouted, "Now King George's army must either drive us from our new fortifications, men, or evacuate by sea!"

"The surprise is complete!" added Knox.

After an interval of stunned silence on the part of the British, the Red Coats began scurrying in every direction along Boston's streets and wharves to man their stations, until every British cannon was manned and primed. Even cannons on board the British ships were readied and sails hoisted as the Brigantines came forward to do battle.

Knox, using the power of his voice via a megaphone, shouted across the bay and down to the British. "Surrender your position and arms or bear the consequences!"

Henry was answered by shipboard cannons opening fire at the Heights, along with more cannon fire coming from the area of the Boston Arsenal.

Some of the American artillery men began to seek cover. "Stand firm, men!" Knox encouraged his cannoneers, Ben and Will among them. "Their cannons cannot possibly reach us here, but we can definitely reach them."

Knox was proven right as the British cannonballs fell short by a hundred yards, making the Americans laugh and mock the Red Coats. Washington, seeing that Henry's predictions had come true, realizing he was correct about where to place the cannons, shouted over the noise, "We have them under our power! They'll have to accept our terms or surrender!" He'd previously sent a dispatch to the opposing general offering him a safe but hasty retreat or to surrender to the Continental Army."

247

Gill McCleary, laughing now at the British, stopped long enough to say to Ben, "All they can do is make noise!" Gill stood in full view of the Red Coats, whose musket fire also fell short, and he was doing a little dance for the enemy soldiers. Seeing this, the other Americans, including Ned, joined in the dance atop Dorchester Heights.

But then Ben heard Knox telling Washington, "They won't listen to reason, General, not until we give them a proper taste of our fire power, sir." Henry was asking to give the order for all the 24-pounders and his beloved 44-pounder to open fire.

Washington, with a solemn nod of his head, gave the go ahead to Knox, adding, "Do what is necessary, Henry, and God grant that it be short-lived, and no civilians are harmed."

The men had already worked to find the range of the ships in the harbor. In a moment, a rain of large iron balls and shot fell all around the three British ships that had dared attempt to get close enough to fire on the Heights. The barrage of fire from the American Artillery sent these ships back and into hiding behind the warehouses and other buildings at the wharves.

Ben and Will helped out at the cannons that stood side-by-side, each young man jumping clear whenever the powder was touched off. Once the ships were safely behind church steeples and rooftops below at Boston, Knox reluctantly ordered that the range be found for the steeples and rooftops. Before long, he made the decision to send a volley to these targets. His men neither questioned him nor hesitated.

"They've got to know we mean business," Henry kept saying to his men up and down the artillery line.

Before it was over, they bombarded the city for most of the day, taking no pleasure in doing so, and anxiously hoping and praying for the British commander to agree to Washington's terms. Finally, General Howe of the British forces was sent word from the General of the Rebel Army, again requesting unconditional surrender or that the British vacate the harbor. Howe had let the day pass, refusing to make any terms with "the *rabble*".

Wind, darkness, and rains came; after a while, Ben could see nothing whatsoever. It was as if Boston—and all her lights—had vanished as a thick fog covered the land. At one point, Ben looked down on the bay, catching a glimpse of white swells that made him recall the time he'd had during his escape from Boston so many months ago. Then he thought he saw something else in the water, possibly a ship, but then it was gone, too.

"Gill, have you still got that telescope of yours?" he asked now.

Gill, beside him, reached into his inside pocket and handed it to Ben. "What're ya gapin' at, son?"

"Not sure yet, maybe it's nothing…but remember how I got across the bay in an open boat…well almost all the way across in a boat?"

"A row boat with one oar, right?"

Ben frowned. "Yes."

"And if you could get as far as you did along the Back Bay area, why not trained soldiers? Is that what you're-a-thinking?"

"If a lot of hands were put on a skiff with oars, hundreds of Red Coats might be right below our position right now, right at this moment, thinking they'll just take the cannons out of our hands."

Ben looked through the telescope through the pea soup fog and somehow caught a glimpse of metal, a belt buckle or a musket, just a glint but enough to know that he was right. He wasted no time in sounding the alarm, shouting, "Red Coats are here on our hill! Just below us!"

Knox, taking Ben at his word, ordered two mortars be primed and fired. Musket fire broke out at the same time as Gill gave the order to fire at the enemy whether seen or not, in the general direction where Ben pointed. The red glow of the mortar shells gave the cannoneers merest glance at the big skiffs, boats taken down from the British ships, filled no to brimming with soldiers. The skiffs could not handle the backwater well, and they'd been unable to reach shore other than at the swamp. The whirlpool effect of the bay, the wind, and the rain had all conspired against the British forces and their ill-fated attempt to come after the artillery by cover of darkness and fog. It stopped the invasion before it could get underway, and when the Continental Army opened fire on the men in the bay, the British scurried back out of sight and out of range.

The failed attempt left Knox's artillerymen laughing, and Knox ordered them to waste no more ammunition on the fog.

"Let the weather have that bunch, boys!" Gill shouted, confirming Knox's wishes.

"You can likely capture the lot of them come dawn, sir," Ben said to Knox. "They'll be threading water and floundering in the mud there in Back Bay."

Gill laughed knowingly and winked at Ben. "Want me to lead a detachment down there, Colonel?" he asked.

Knox replied, "At dawn...just to make sure their little operation continues to be a failure."

CHAPTER EIGHTEEN

The attempt made by boat, by night from the bay, in thick fog proved the only response from General Howe. The only response thus far he'd given General Washington, and although Howe had lost some men in the attempt to strike at the Continental Cannoneers, he still held out. For thirteen more days he held out while hourly bombardments hit his fortifications and kept his ships out to sea. The guns of Ticonderoga had by then annihilated the old Customs House, the courthouse, all manner of shops—including Knox's bookstore. Church steeples and rooftops had been set aflame.

The bombardment had begun awkwardly, the men training on the job, so to speak. The gunners were untried, still learning their weapons and their way, but they soon began to hit their marks, and each time they did, a rousing cheer followed. They soon had the ability to strike with deadly accuracy, knocking out as many military installations as Knox could plot a trajectory for. His bookstore had not been a casual decision, but intelligence had reported that it, like so many other businesses, was used to house Red Coats—or Lobster Backs as the local fisherman had always called them.

With each firing off of a cannon, Ben Cross alternated between cheering and cringing, for one ball went straight into the ship-building yards where Mr. Gray and no doubt Wilbur kept vigil. Besides, it was hard in general to watch his hometown being destroyed piece by piece using the guns meant to save Boston.

At dawn on March 17th, St. Patrick's Day, the cannoneers celebrated around their fires. Knox allowing mild drinking in the ranks, understanding the needs of the men in his command, most of whom were of Irish descent. In the midst of songs and dancing, men pairing into dancing partners here and there, the monotony of camp life was broken. And amid the celebrations of St. Patrick's Day, a messenger from General Washington rode into camp, shouting, "They're leaving! The Red Coats are evacuating! They refuse to surrender, but they're turning tail and running!"

Knox called up to the horseback rider and once he verified the report, reading it in Washington's handwriting, he shouted to the guard at the fortifications. "Do you see any sign that this is true, Effram!"

Effram had already been scanning the city to determine just that, using a field telescope. "They've brought their ships outta hiding, and the men are boarding them, sir! Lots of red-faced soldiers, sir!"

Gill shouted back to Knox after searching the harbor, "Sir, do you want us to fire on them, goose them out of there?"

"No! No firing, Sergeant! Not until I learn of General Washington's wishes."

Knox mounted his horse and rode for Cambridge to report directly to Washington on what they were witnessing. While Henry was away, Ben,

William, and Gill, along with Ned, Effram, and the other cannoneers, watched while General Howe's entire command boarded the fleet of ships that had held Boston Harbor in its grip for nearly a year now. Hundreds of Tory citizens, fearing retribution— including Lucy's parents—were also being boarded, leaving the city for a group of nearby islands far out of cannon fire range where they might plot a course for the British held islands of the West Indies, Barbados in particular, if not Quebec, Canada. The Cannoneers were taking bets on the destination of the ships, and the scuttlebutt presumed it would most likely be Canada. No one knew for certain of General Howe's destination, but Gill surmised aloud, "Canada because they have a strong foothold there." Still others wildly guessed that they would next strike at the port city of New York to set up shop there. This seemed highly unlikely according to Gill. "Barbados for the citizens, then Canada for the soldiers," he told Ben.

Whatever their final destination, the British fleet had regrouped with all aboard. Each vastly overcrowded ship flew the Union Jack, the flag fluttering in the ocean breeze. Each ship also sat low in the water from the weight of their cargo, cannons, soldiers, and civilians.

The cannoneers watched as one-by-one each ship made its way further out to sea, the whole operation done with the characteristic ease and efficiency of the British Navy. Ben certainly thought so. thought. For all intents and purposes, the city of Boston had been set free.

Nobody actually knew what the British plans were, but the Americans needed no plans to ride into Boston behind General George Washington, vindicated and victorious. Soldiers and civilians alike cheered up and down Long Street as Washington's officers—Henry among them—proudly paraded over the Neck and into Boston.

Young Colonel Henry Knox, rising alongside Washington, waved his hat wildly overhead, waving to friends and citizens who had lived through Howe's occupation and Washington's bombardment. Several who knew Knox well began chanting his nickname, "Ox! Ox! Welcome home!"

Ben and William rode horses as well and waved to the crowd cheering them on. They greeted hungry, emaciated, weary Bostonians with a wagon loaded down with bread, fresh vegetables, and meats—all of which Ben and the others happily doled out to those in need. The foodstuff had been commandeered by order of the general, confiscated from camp vendors and merchants. As Ben was passing out food by the armful, he heard someone calling his name, and he instantly recognized the unmistakable voice of Wilbur Gilford.

Wilbur was pushing through the crowd, and Ben, now atop the food wagon, leapt down to greet his old friend. He hardly recognized the slimmed down Wilbur. Shouting one another's names, the boys hugged. "Ben, it's really you! They told us the soldiers had killed you and left your body to rot in the swamp!"

"They lied, Wilbur! The reports of my death were to keep others like you from trying to escape

255

the city. Sure I've been froze near to death but not shot by any Red Coat."

"I wish we'd known, Mr. Gray and me. He was so hurt at losing you, Ben."

"Where is he?"

"Sorry to tell you, but he caught something bad, fell ill…and he never recovered."

"He's gone? Passed away?"

Wilbur gave him a tearful nod. "Afraid so."

"So you've been on your own for how long?"

"Last few months."

"I was with the Knox artillery train the whole way…all the way up to Fort Ticonderoga and back again with the guns—the cannons!"

"What an adventure that must've been!"

"I'll never forget it, ever."

"That makes you a hero, Ben."

"*Nahhh…*"

"Sure it does. All the talk is about the Knox train. Wow, Ben Cross helped save Boston."

Ben blushed. "I had plenty of help, Wilbur. But hey, you look awful thin!"

He patted his stomach. "Dropped some weight, for sure. A starvation diet will do that to ya."

Ben shouted for Ned to toss him a loaf of bread, which he handed to Wilbur. "Eat."

They found a blackened, smashed wall where a cannonball had torn into it, and it made for a curious bench now. They sat, and Wilbur tore into the bread. Ben solemnly said, "It hurts me something awful that Mr. Gray's no longer with us."

"Me too. I've had time to heal over it some, but for you it's *new* news. But you know, Ben, he loved the two of us like we were his boys, his sons."

"Yeah…called us brothers, remember? Ha!"

"We are kinda like brothers, Ben, and now we're partners."

"Partners?"

"In business."

"You're not making sense, Wilbur."

"Mr. Gray, he wrote out a will at the end, Ben…a will that leaves his entire holdings, the whole shipyard to you and to me as equal partners."

Ben stared down the street to see the Old North Church completely gone, mere taters remaining, not so much as a skeletal hull of its former existence showing. His first thought was that the Old Sow had done this. But suddenly at his side stood Knox, William beside him. "We didn't do that much damage, Ben. The church was stripped for firewood like my store and all the other buildings. It's a wonder the steeple remained. That part was us."

Ben saw the empty space where Knox's bookstore had once stood—also scavenged for its wooden walls. "I'm feeling an overwhelming need to go stare out at the ocean," Ben said now. "I sure don't want to see what they've done to our shipyard."

Wilbur chimed in with, "It'll take years to get it back to where it had been, but we can do it together, Ben. I know we can."

They found the shipyard nearly as empty and as useless as Colonel Knox's ruined bookstore. Ben's excitement at their having taken Boston, all the parading, cheering, and sharing faded as his face fell on seeing the destroyed shipyard. Seeing how badly Ben was taking it, Wilbur said, "We can rebuild her, Ben. We can get a loan…and together we can bring the yard back to its former glory."

"Perhaps after the war, Wilbur, but you see this uniform I'm wearing? Well…I've signed on for the long haul as a Knox artilleryman."

"You sure have grown a whole lot since that night on the wharf when you escaped, Ben."

"I might not have made it, if you'd not distracted the soldiers for me, Wilbur. I hated seeing you caught and having to go on without you."

"I knew that, Ben. Have known it all these months."

Ben had to step away from the ruined shipyard. With bowed head, he meandered toward the wharves and the equally destroyed Customs House, and finally to what had been the British Arsenal where he again encountered Henry and William Knox. Colonel Knox, seeing Ben, said, "I am anxious to see what, if anything, General Howe left in his hasty retreat in the way of artillery and shot."

To their combined delight, they entered the stone building, which had been the city jail, only to discover that Howe had left behind hundreds of artillery pieces; most were howitzers and mortars, but many were large caliber guns. Some had been spiked and their trunnions knocked off with sledge hammers. "No bother. A good Massachusetts gunsmith can rebuild these cannon to be like new."

"Just overnight the First American Artillery Train has doubled in size," added Ben, brightening at the realization.

"And look at this corner!" added Will, pointing at tons of gunpowder, cannonballs, and grape shot left in the wake of the retreating army. Ammunition the British might easily have destroyed by dumping it into the ocean.

"Well now, boys, we know what to do with this stash, don't we?"

Together they laughed at this, and Wilbur, who'd entered behind them, laughed along with Ben, glad to see he was feeling better.

The Bostonians, so long cut off from her waterways by the British and land routes by the American forces, had suffered immeasurably from hunger and sickness. Their having taken Boston back from the hands of the British made them all heroes. This show of strength won over any remaining Tories and fence-sitters, as did the flour, vegetables, meats, and doctors that the Continental Army brought with it. For months afterward, Boston still looked like an occupied city, and Bostonians lived amid the rubble, but everyone also knew freedom. The ten-month long Siege of Boston was over, and it had come to a good end.

Several days later, after all the ceremonies and cheers had died away and faded, Ben was summoned to General George Washington's new headquarters in Boston, formerly occupied by Howe. As Ben made his way to the general's office, he thought of the last words he'd heard from

Washington at the public square while in mid-speech to the cheering crowds. Washington had said, "There has never been a cause for war so important as that of the American people's cause here in this fight."

Ben and every other American soldier realized that the Battle for Boston was the natural conclusion in a struggle that had begun at Lexington and Concord, continued at Bunker Hill, and had settled into the months' long siege until finally every soldier of King George of Great Britain was gone from the Massachusetts Bay Colony. They also knew that the war would go on, and next time the British would be unlikely to take the Continental soldiers for a pack of disorganized and disgruntled farmers.

For now, the troops were jubilant at the recent news that they would be moving out for New York City to protect her harbor from any possible British invasion there. And now for some mysterious reason, General Washington had called for Ben at his headquarters, where he stood on the stone steps about to enter. From a tavern down the street, he thought he heard Gill, Ned, and others singing a victory song. The headquarters had been the home of a wealthy sympathizer to the British cause, the Tory having welcomed Howe to set up shop in his home. He and his family were likely with Howe now in Canada, Ben imagined. Ben announced who he was to the guards and they'd been instructed to let him pass. He had never been inside such a palatial home in his life, and he felt ill-at-ease, as if a thief who'd snuck in through a back window…as if he did not belong.

One of Washington's wait staff led him through a maze of rooms until finally they came upon Washington, looking tired as he studied maps spread across a huge, beautiful desk. When he saw Ben had entered, Washington smiled wide and said, "Private Cross! Wonderful, come forward; have a seat. So good of you to come."

Ben thought but did not say: *What else can a soldier do but come when his general asks him to?* Instead, he returned the general's smile and found a seat, curious yet as to why he had been summoned.

"Ben, Colonel Knox has told me about that shipyard you and another Boston lad inherited."

"You want to buy it off our hands? It's a shambles, sir."

"So I've heard." Washington came around his desk and leaned against it, and bowed toward Ben from his great height. "I know I can be intimidating, Ben, but please, relax."

"Yes, sir."

"At ease, soldier."

Ben finally relaxed his body but not his mind. Then Washington said, "Ben, I know of no one in Boston in any position to help with that yard, either to invest money or time into it's getting up and running again."

"You're so right about that, sir."

Washington held a big hand up to Ben to silence him. "I know, Ben."

"Not a soul in his right mind, sir would—"

"*Ahh-ahh*!" Washington again signaled for silence. "Hear me out. Colonel Knox tells me that with a little capital, you and your partner, Gilford is it? That you two could return it to a thriving business."

"General, you…you have an army to run, a war to fight. I-I don't understand why you should worry about that pile of rubble at the wharves, sir…respectfully."

"Is it not true, what they say about you, Ben?"

"What's that, sir?"

"That you and your business partner, Wilbur Gilford, could make first-rate shipmasters, like Mr. Gray, who I presume, taught you well?"

"Well…yes, sir, but with a war going on—"

"With a war going on, Ben—" interrupted Washington—"the Continental Navy needs building, and from what Knox tells me, you could be a significant part of that effort here in Boston."

Ben swallowed hard. "*Ahhh*…I don't know about that, sir. I planned to remain with the artillery."

"To have a proper navy, Ben, we require ships—a fleet of ships that can out-maneuver the British warships." Washington paced before Ben now, a man who towered over everyone in his presence. He then placed a firm hand on Ben's shoulder. "What would you say to a government contract to build the ships we need, Ben? Do you think you could employ enough men at your shipyard to supply us with what is needed?"

262

"I…I am sure that if we had the funds, the startup funds we could…but aren't there ships already in service, like The Finn Hawk?"

"Most of the privateers like the Hawk, Ben, have been seized by local municipalities and colonies south of us to protect their harbors along the seaboard."

"There is no Continental Navy to speak of then?"

"Exactly. You know what troubles we've had uniting the colonies to stand against Great Britain, Ben…how much effort has gone into creating a cohesive army and governing body. You have seen much of it firsthand now, both in and around Cambridge. Just imagine what little cooperation I am likely to get if I attempt to organize all the private ships into a single fighting force?"

"I see your point, sir."

"I am asking you to continue using your skills, just as Captain Blaylock is using his privateer, and Colonel Knox is using his with the artillery. At the same time, you will be building ships for the cause of freedom, you will be building a reputation as a reliable businessman."

"We could make Gray's Shipyard mean something in Boston again," Ben said, thinking of the possibilities. "I would like to do it for Mr. Gray, sir."

"Will it be Cross and Gilford Shipyard or Gilford and Cross Shipyard?" asked the general.

"Neither. It'll stay Gray's Shipyard."

"When can we get some startup funds, sir?"

263

"Between you and me, son, the congress has to find these funds. Without a navy, our revolution is....pardon the pun, dead in the water, and they have to understand that this is an expense we cannot count on Henry Knox's backing for! They still owe him for the artillery train he's created of thin air!"

"I see."

"Don't expect ready payment for years, Ben, but for now, operating capital only. It's likely the best we can do. Your and Gilford's efforts will largely be done out of pride in your work and patriotism, but eventually, you will be rewarded monetarily."

Ben shook hands with the general when Washington extended his hand, sealing the deal. Ben, smiling, said, "First order of business is to hang out a sign, and I know a fellow who does good work for that."

Ben started away, but Washington stopped him, saying, "There is one more thing, Ben."

Ben wheeled and saw that the general held up a large gold medallion on a ribbon, the light gleaming off the medal. "What's this?"

"Call it due reward for a frightened young fellow, who left my office many months ago to go on an incredible journey and to return a man. It's yours, Ben. Young Will Knox and Gill McCleary have also received this medal of honor from my hand."

Ben bowed his head and Washington placed the medallion around his neck. "In Philadelphia, the Continental Congress authorized the medal be made in honor of our taking Boston back from those *ahhh...Lobster Backs*!"

Ben stared at the insignia on the medal. It was the first American coin medallion minted by the new congress. Lifting the surface to his eyes, Ben studied the workmanship: a vivid depiction of Washington and officers watching the departure of British ships. In the middle-distance, stood the American troops and the artillery—the Guns of Ticonderoga. Ben beamed at this.

"Cherish it, take pride in it for your part in our struggle, Ben, and now as shipmaster, carry on for the cause."

Ben was speechless. He left the general's headquarters in a daze. Once outside, he stood on the quiet cobblestone street beneath the glow of lights from windows on both sides of the path pointed the way back to the wharves, where he hoped to find Wilbur and relay the wonderful news, Ben suddenly gave out with a war-whoop that would have made Gill and Ned tremble, then he raced to the wharves in search of Wilbur, his medal bouncing hard against his chest as he pounded over the wooden sidewalks. In his ear, he kept hearing Washington's words: "Take pride in it..."

"I intend to, General Washington! Colonel Knox! I intend to!" Ben felt certain that he owed his newfound life and future to Henry.

EPILOGUE

On the 4th of July of 1776, the Declaration of Independence was read in every public square, town hall, commons, and gathering place of the first United States. Having been adopted by the Continental Congress, this declaration was the first formal Declaration of War made against Great Britain.

Colonel Henry Knox and his artillery regiment first heard the document while in New York City, where the Continental Army was now bivouacked, awaiting further action. Before long, the American forces saw a great deal of action and had many difficult years in which defeat was followed by defeat. During these years, Colonel Knox rose to the rank of Major General, and his artillery regiment continued to serve under Washington in every major engagement of the Revolutionary War, also known as the *War of Independence*.

However, as with most wars, this one lingered on as predicted by both Knox and Washington; it lingered on until October 19th, 1781—five years *after* the signing of the Declaration of Independence. On this historic day, George Washington's forces conquered the last seaport city held by the Red Coats that offered a supply line supporting British forces in America—a place named Yorktown, Virginia. The lessons learned at the Siege of Boston were still being used by Knox and Washington.

At Yorktown, British General Charles Cornwallis found himself surrounded and surprised by American troops, a French fleet (the French having come into the war on the side of the Americans), and the American Artillery led by Knox. The Guns of Ticonderoga were still firing, the Old Sow among them.

At the close of war, young Ben Cross was twenty-two and enjoying a reputation as a master ship builder along with Wilbur. At Gray's Shipyard in Boston Harbor, he heard sudden jubilation erupt among the workmen, heralding the news that the British flag had been taken down at Yorktown and replaced with an American flag, and that terms of surrender had once again sent the British packing—*this time for good.* The years' long war was finally over, and America had won her independence.

Among the revelers now, Ben thought of a day nearly six years before when he had been taken in as a 'prisoner' by Ned Bottomly and Gill McCleary, marched into a wretched camp of disjointed soldiers with no uniforms, no flag, and no artillery! It appeared the Continental Army had changed the natural order of the universe—or at least the order in which kings placed their faith upon. It overturned the world-held belief and notion that people could be ruled by Kings who supposedly held a Divine Right to govern. Like dominoes other countries found their own independence from a feudal system that had been in place for centuries.

Ben and his shipyard workers were disappointed later, however, to learn of the British return. The surrender at Yorktown had so looked like the final blow to the British, but unfortunately, the struggle to hold on was too great for King George to relinquish. The war dragged on for yet another two years after Yorktown had fallen to the Americans. It was only after a number of other clashes between the two forces that a formal Peace Treaty was ratified, signed, sealed, and delivered.

After the war was finally over, Major General Henry Knox became the First Secretary of War to the United States of America under President George Washington. Knox, who had built so many fortifications over the war years, now busily worked to build fortifications for a new nation, primarily monetary ones. Lucy joined him in his new life, continuing to support him as she did throughout the war years. His brother, William, returned to Boston and became a prominent businessman, investing in such companies as Gray's Shipyard, among other lucrative establishments as Boston rebuilt.

Gray's Shipyard weathered the war years in hardship, but it would have been far worse under anyone's management but Wilbur's and Ben's. Even so, the yard fell heavily in debt as a result of filling Congressional contracts, as Congress took a long time in paying its debts. Even when Congress managed to pay off a debt, the Congressional Dollar proved to be nearly worthless. Still, with Will Knox's help, the years following the war saw an upswing in business as the shipyard branched out. Wilbur and Ben had established a fleet of merchant ships of their own—many being decommissioned from the Continental Navy as recompense! Soon their fleet was operating with steady trade agreements between themselves and businessmen in the West Indies, Spain, France, China, and even in Great Britain—the former *enemy*.

One day at a tavern over ale, Will Knox confessed to Ben that Congress—even after all that Henry had done, had still not reimbursed him for his costs in financing the incredible Ticonderoga trek. "What's Henry going to do about it?" asked Ben.

Will frowned. "He laughs it off! He takes it in his usual good fashion. Tells me that one day, the country will be strong, and then our congress will repay all her debts. I have my doubts. They are terrible businessmen, that lot. I fear our debts overseas will never be paid!"

As Ben grew further into manhood, he made several trips back and forth across the seas, and even once made it to China. His shipyard flourished along with his and Wilbur's reputations, but for all of Ben Cross' successes in life, he never boasted on any save one: how he had played a part in making the First American Artillery train a reality.

The End *of this story...*

About The Author

Robert W. Walker has many other historical novels and alternate historical novels: Annie's War, Children of Salem, City for Ransom (and its 2 sequels) as well as Titanic 2012, and Bismarck 2013. Walker is also the author of some forty crime novels. All of his works can be found on Amazon.com/Kindle books, and many are also available as audio books via Audible.com.

Walker himself can be reached for comment at his website: www.robertwalkerbooks.com and he maintains a presence on Twitter and Facebook.